Bloody Waters

Immigrants, Mariners, and Misfits
Clash in the Florida Keys

JOHN GORDON

DEDICATION

To my family...past, present, and future.

FLORIDA
MIAMI
FLORIDA KEYS
KEY LARGO
KEY WEST
HAVANA
CUBA

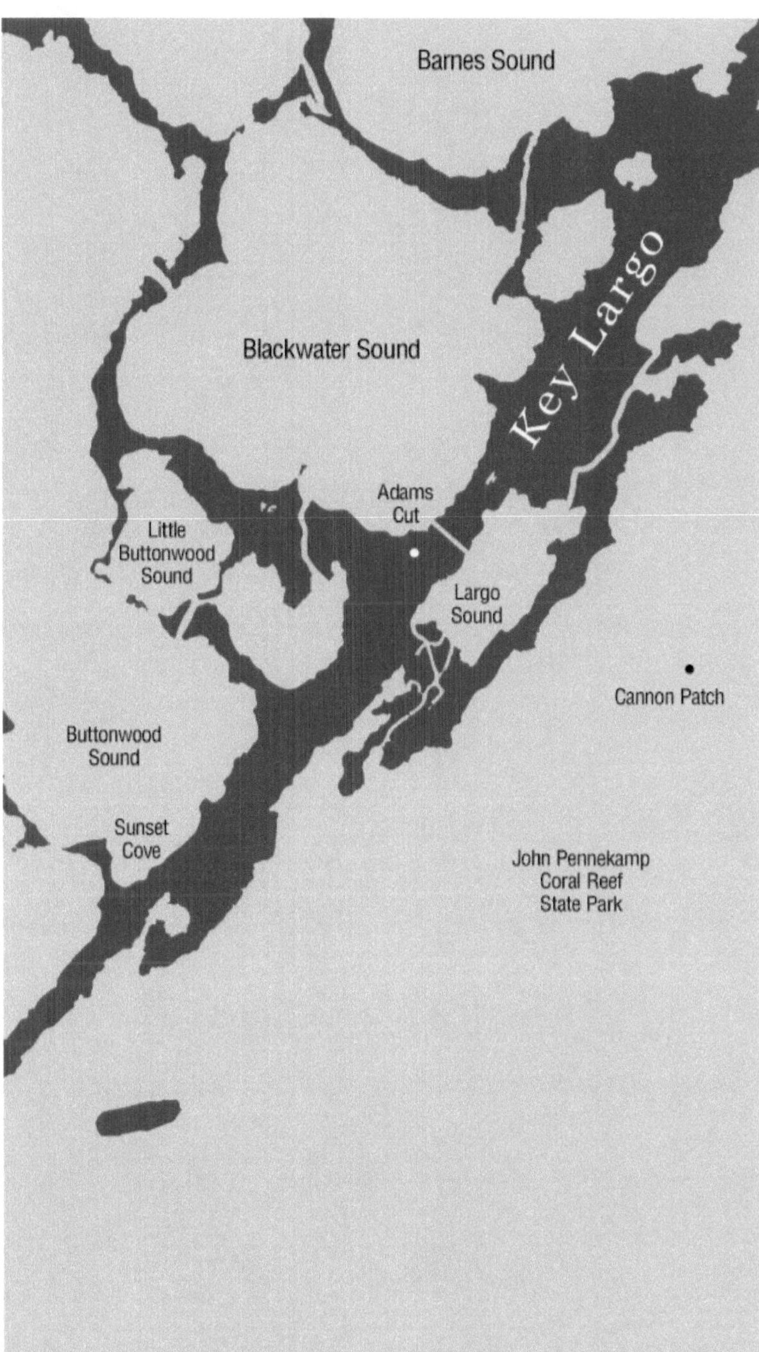

Barnes Sound
Blackwater Sound
Key Largo
Adams Cut
Little Buttonwood Sound
Largo Sound
Cannon Patch
Buttonwood Sound
Sunset Cove
John Pennekamp Coral Reef State Park

John Gordon

CHAPTER ONE

Ed Melnik placed the pistol on the floor. He retrieved the chair that only seconds ago was his adversary's apparent weapon of choice.

"Someone call the County Sheriff," he said calmly. "I'm not goin' anywhere."

The other patrons at DJs Diner began to stir, some frantically, others sloth-slowly. A couple nervous men attempted to assist Carlos, the victim. His motionless body and the expanding pool of blood on the scuffed, yellow tile floor signalled he was gone. The head-shot was lethal.

"Y'all saw what happened," Ed shouted. "We were arguing. He came at me swinging a chair. I was in fear for my life or maybe a bad injury. I was packing, legally—<u>legally</u> mind you. I'm <u>always</u> packing, and I defended myself here tonight per the Florida statute. It's not my fault this clown lost his cool."

Ed recited the events in a manner that eerily and accurately reflected Florida's stand-your-ground law. He didn't claim to be cornered, trapped without an exit. He didn't need to; that aspect of the law had been tossed fifteen years prior. Ed also pointed out that DJs is a restaurant, not a bar. He knew that concealed carry in a bar was not allowed.

Although they were shaken and wanted to bolt, several witnesses stayed around until law enforcement arrived. The officers took their statements. Ed calmly provided his description of the confrontation, and the witnesses confirmed his story. Eventually, Carlos' body was removed by the coroner.

Ed was arrested and held without bail pending an investigation of the incident. He was cleared and freed in eight days. He celebrated that night at the Sea Breeze Motel with a bottle of Captain Morgan rum and a plump, aging hooker.

CHAPTER TWO

SUNDAY, EIGHT WEEKS LATER

As their American Airlines flight skidded onto the sizzling Miami runway, Jackson Boyd and Art Pritchard exhaled loudly. They had been in transit from San Francisco for sixteen miserable hours; their wrinkled polo shirts and sleepy faces were testaments to the grueling trip.

"That creative air route cost us two layovers, a runway delay and a thunderstorm over Shreveport," said Jackson. "If that's how you always get to Miami, you need to strangle your travel agent."

"Jackie, she is my cousin's wife. I think I am one of her last clients," Art said in a pleading voice. "I can't show my face at the next reunion if I fire her. Come to think of it, I swore to avoid those gatherings; happy family members brag and the miserable ones complain. Consider it done."

The pair deplaned and walked through the maze of Miami International Airport's hallways, deadends, and shortcuts. Fortunately, Art knew the drill.

"Now I see why this airport's station code is MIA," Jackson said. "Jimmy Hoffa is not dead; he is probably just lost in here somewhere."

"Jackie, we…"

Jackson interrupted with more sarcasm. "Is Tom Hanks still filming *The Terminal* here?"

"Jackson, I know you are tired, but let's not start a week in Florida like this, okay?"

Jackson nodded and kept walking. They cut through the baggage claim area; there was no need to stop. Each had brought only a soft-sided carry on case. Their next stop was the car rental center, but that was a half-mile away. As they followed the herd onward, Jackson started up again.

"Art, are we <u>walking</u> to Key Largo from here? You know we have a tight deadline, right?"

Art said nothing, but of course he hadn't forgotten about Jackson's speaking gig later that afternoon. Art had arranged it. Even though they <u>were</u> in a time squeeze, Art thought Jackson was being uncharacteristically prickly. Art promptly wrote off Jackson's "bitchies" to the shitty day of travel they had just endured. *He's cranky now, but he's gonna love Key Largo and the warm water boating there.*

Compared to the airline's miniscule seats, the tired, white, Hyundai Tucson rental SUV was plenty comfortable during the forty-minute ride south to Florida City. Jackson dozed off. Art pulled into the last fuel stop before hitting the "stretch" on Highway 1—an uninhabited patch of marshland between Florida City and the top of the Keys.

Jackson awoke with a start. He was hungry, and his stomach was rumbling. Before the trip, he scoured WebMD and concluded he had a peptic ulcer. He booked an appointment for the following week; he hoped his internist would confirm his self-diagnosis and figure out a solution. In the meantime, Jackson was avoiding acidic foods and alcohol. He wasn't very good at the "avoiding" part. Art was sympathetic about Jackson's stomach issues.

"Yo, Art. Your house looks like a big-ass filling station."

"We are stopping quickly for snacks and food, Jackie. We've gotta keep moving once we get to my place. Glad you caught a few winks."

"Lunch at the RaceTrac gas station and gourmet kitchen. You <u>did</u> say the food here was cheap and tasty. Can't wait," said Jackson."

They entered and checked out the choices: warm faux McSandwiches, rolling six-week-old hot dogs, and packaged junk foods of all breeds. They went with the McChokers for immediate consumption, then they selected a few groceries for the house—milk, cereal, eggs, bread, cheese, salami and beer.

Jackson commented, "I will try to avoid the beer. Maybe we don't need it?" It was a passive-aggressive way for Jackson to say, "Please don't tempt me with beer."

Art pointed out, "It would seem impossible to come to RaceTrac and <u>not</u> buy beer. Look at those four deck-to-ceiling beverage coolers against the wall. They are labeled BEER, BEER, MORE BEER, and ENDLESS BEER."

After a supportive nod from Jackson, Art paid for groceries and the case of Kalik Bahamian Beer. It seemed like a good way to get into the island mood. Jackson paid, they remounted the Tucson, and as they rocketed down "The Stretch," each wolfed down two of the tepid, premade sandwiches. Thirty-five minutes later, the Hyundai rolled into Art's visitor parking area. There was a crunching sound coming from the surface beneath the tires.

"What is that stuff?" asked Jackson.

"It's chunks of coral that have been ground to a uniform size. It's called pea rock; mine are about one-half inch in diameter which is typical. It's used here everywhere as a quick surface for driveways and parking lots, and it's popular because it allows water to drain while maintaining a nice surface with good traction." Jackson gave an approving look.

Art parked the SUV in the carport under the house. They grabbed their bags and climbed the stairs to the main door for Art's airy, white-trimmed, yellow dockside house in the Pirate's Cove section of Key Largo. Art welcomed Jackson officially, then he attended to his arrival checklist. Jackson toured the house. He dropped off his bag in his guest room. The room was painted cool blue and like everywhere else in the house, it had nautical themed paintings on the walls. There was a photo of Jackson's extended family on the white dresser and full-sized Venetian blinds over the big window.

The main area of the house including the living room, dining area and kitchen reflected an open floor plan. The light-filled living room had white sofas and nautical-style tables facing the sliders and massive windows; all that glass provided a 180-degree view of Buttonwood Sound to the north and Sunset Cove to the east. It was a perspective every mariner dreamed of.

A stylishly rusted, four-foot-diameter compass rose hung on the east wall next to a large window that welcomed the rising sun each morning. There was a large mirror with a cherry wood sunburst frame hanging on the west wall adjacent to a smaller window. Nautical artifacts, boat pictures and ocean scenes filled in wall space and decorated an enormous white bookshelf on the living room's back wall. Art had nicely created a "luxury beach house" ambiance.

Jackson went downstairs to see the grounds, garage, boat gear room, and the forty-foot dock where the boat was tied up. The waterside "backyard" consisted of a large patch of pea rock rimmed by acacia, buttonwood and key lime trees. There was a stone seating area and a professional-quality barbecue unit beneath the balcony.

Art's pale green boat, *Jenny Girl*, was perched atop an electric hoist. Its smooth, bright keel hovered four feet above the waterline. Jackson was impressed with the boat setup. *Smart. No bottom paint needed to discourage clinging sea critters. Otherwise, a week in this warm water, and the hull would look like a marine science project.*

From the long, pale blue Trex dock, Jackson gazed into the distance. The clear, turquoise water looked fabulous, especially when compared to the murky brown water of San Francisco Bay. There was a scrub of bright green mangrove about a mile out. Further in the distance Jackson could see sets of red and green channel markers. Even further to the northwest, he saw part of the lush

Everglades National Park. *What a fabulous nautical playground. No wonder boaters flock here; it is heaven.*

Art's voice cracked the calm. From the upstairs patio, he said, "Jackie, we gotta keep moving. We're due at the Lions Club in an hour. You are the star, so we can't be late. Get out of your stinky travel suit, grab a shower and let's go."

Jackson sniffed his armpits. "Damn," he muttered, then he hustled upstairs for a shave and a shower. After the shower, he had a Kalik, which mellowed his mood. At that moment, Jackson much preferred to lounge on the deck versus going to the den of Lions. Travel at age seventy-five took a greater toll than when he was younger. During the short drive to the Lions Club, Jackson asked Art again why he had arranged this event.

"Jackie," Art said, "this is a nautical community, and they love hearing unique stories from boaters. Our little 'adventure' with the terrorists in San Francisco a few years back made big news even here. Plus, the local clubs are always looking for speakers. I nominated you. Be proud."

Jackson responded. "Yeah, I did that talk around the Bay Area for about six months: yacht clubs, Power Squadrons, the Coast Guard and veterans groups. I tried to not make it about me. It was really about <u>us</u> Coast Guard volunteers and the really useful training we got to put into action."

"Jackson, we have had this chat before. People need heroes, and you stepped up when it mattered. Just roll with it, okay?"

"Heck," said Jackson, "you were there and did just as much as me. Anyway, I hope I don't screw it up tonight. Between jet lag, my gurgling belly and Mr. Kalik, I'm fading."

John Gordon

CHAPTER THREE

Art turned the Hyundai into the club's parking lot. "Well, there's the Lion's den. You all set?"

Jackson chuckled as he responded. "Your 'regional hero of modest fame' is locked and loaded, maybe too loaded."

Art gave him a thumbs up before both men climbed out of the car. The rustic Lions Club was abuzz. It was clear the bar had been busy for hours. Word was that in addition to doing good work, the Lions, as with many civic club members, also knew how to party.

Art and Jackson were welcomed as though they were regulars. Soon, "Tom," a permanently tanned, middle-aged man in a Hawaiian shirt, khaki shorts and weather-worn top-siders—the Keys uniform —introduced himself and offered his welcome.

Art pointed to Jackson and said to Tom, "He is your program tonight. Can we loosen him up with a drink?" By that time, Jackson was already feeling better about his upcoming talk, but the drink sounded good. Tom retrieved a couple rum and Cokes.

Tom announced—he shouted—to the crowd that the program was about to start, and he asked the folks in the bar to take seats in the adjoining room. A few people moaned their disapproval, but everyone complied. Jackson concluded that he'd better keep his remarks brief. After a half hour away from the bar, some of the Lions were sure to turn on him. But for now, it was "show time."

The meeting room was the size of a double garage. Ancient, stackable black chairs had been set out for the audience; on any given Friday night, the room would be a cozy dance hall with bad acoustics. Photographs of club officers and previous events hung randomly on the stark white walls. Stuffed fish trophies were also hanging here and there. A curious, disintegrating straw hat was mounted behind the portable podium.

After the attendees settled, Tom walked to the podium and called the room to attention. His prepared introduction was mercifully brief but excessive, gushy. One would think that Jackson had taken Iwo Jima by himself back in 1945.

"Our guest tonight is a true American hero," Tom began. "His actions in San Francisco on October 11th, 2017 are well documented and appropriately heralded. He was the 'tip of the spear' that day, risking everything while facing down terrorists bent on killing hundreds and causing an ecological disaster of epic proportions. Tonight we are honored to hear the story, first hand, from that man. Ladies and gentlemen, it is my honor to introduce to you, Mr. Jackson Boyd."

The crowd offered polite applause. Jackson set down his empty glass and stepped to the podium. He looked fresh, handsome and fit. The first thing he did was walk back Tom's praise.

"Thank you, Tom, and thanks to the rest of you for coming out tonight."

He continued. "Before getting into the details, I need to make it clear that I am an ordinary guy who happened to recieve, <u>accidentally</u>, some critical information while a serious problem was playing out on San Francisco Bay. As of today, there are 24,000 Coast Guard Auxiliarists like me, volunteers who would have done exactly what I did if they had that information.

"Also," he continued, "I didn't confront the terrorists alone. Other Coast Guard Auxiliarists on my boat and on other boats from my Division became part of the solution. My primary crewmember and indispensable partner that day, Art Pritchard, is sitting right over there. You need to know that Art is a highly decorated Army Ranger, a Vietnam veteran, <u>and</u> a retired Sheriff's Captain. He is also a homeowner here in Key Largo. Please show <u>that</u> fine man your appreciation for his tremendous service to this country."

Art was sitting to the left of the podium. He stood, smiled and nodded to the group. The attendees applauded loudly, then even louder. Soon the audience stood as they recognized Art. He was embarrassed; Jackson was delighted. Jackson had always known that Art was a far braver man than him.

Jackson then told the story of the now famous, attempted terrorist attack on San Francisco. Despite the beers and rum, Jackson's words flowed like a well-modulated recording.

"Three bored and bitter young men from Iowa—their leader called himself 'Hamit'—posed as adventurous travelers aboard the oil tanker *Gemini* sailing from Valdez, Alaska to San Francisco. The ship was huge: nearly as long as three football fields. Her capable captain was Karl Johansson.

"During the voyage, however, those Iowa boys brutally abused the other three paying passengers and the nine crewmembers. They eventually commandeered the ship using the handguns they smuggled aboard. Their plan was to use the massive vessel to commit a terrorist act in San Francisco. They were deadly serious; as the ship approached its destination, they murdered an innocent man on board.

"*Gemini* was scheduled to arrive in San Francisco during a busy Sunday Fleet Week event—an annual spectacle featuring a parade of famous ships and aerial performances including the Blue Angels. Thousands of spectators would be at the waterfront, a 'target rich environment' as they say. Hamit's plan was to ram the popular and crowded dockside shopping center, Pier 39."

Jackson digressed to lay some groundwork. "I need to back up for a second. Before going to Alaska to get aboard *Gemini*, the three Iowa boys spent time in the Bay Area, basically doing reconnaissance. The leader of the group, using his actual Christian name, took a ride on my boat, I'm sorry to say. That's a <u>very</u> curious part of this whole saga.

"A month prior to Fleet Week, he rented a junky boat, and it lost power. He called the Coast Guard for help. His rescue vessel that day was my boat, *Salt Shaker*. Art and I happened to be on Coast Guard Auxiliary duty, and we took his disabled vessel in tow and delivered it to a marina dock nearby.

"At the dock, Art and I completed a written report, and I gave the skipper my contact information. He told me his name was Daniel Stinson. He claimed to be interested in joining the Coast Guard Auxiliary. A few days later, Stinson called me, and we arranged a time for him to ride along during an Auxiliary patrol. After that call, I had Stinson's cell number saved in my mobile phone.

"On the day of the Auxiliary patrol, Art and I were frustrated when Stinson was a no-show at the departure dock. So, I called his cell phone. Stinson said he was on his way and would be there 'ricky-tick'. He eventually turned up, and we left the marina. During the patrol, he was far more interested in the bridges and the waterfront than Auxiliary boat duties and protocols. Neither Art nor I appreciated being used as tour guides, so we agreed to avoid Stinson in the future."

Jackson's story returned to the day of the confrontation. "Now back to October 11th. During the airshow I mentioned earlier, *Gemini* was on approach to San Francisco. Disregarding the hundreds of small boats on the Bay, Hamit, the hijacker, demanded that Captain Johansson slow the ship, steer it under the Golden Gate Bridge, then bring it to a stop in the center of the Bay, about four miles offshore. When the ship was nearly dead in the water, Hamit instructed Johansson to turn the vessel ninety degrees to starboard, toward the bustling waterfront.

"Hamit used the ship's VHF radio to announce his intentions on channel 21-Alpha to the Coast Guard and anyone else listening. I guess Hamit figured it was too late for the Coasties or law enforcement to respond, and he wanted to declare some kind of bogus 'glory' before slamming the dock and killing hundreds.

"Art here, a fella named Steve Osmond and I were on duty that day. *Salt Shaker*, my boat, was perhaps a mile from Pier 39 when *Gemini* made its turn. Like many others monitoring the Coast Guard's primary operations radio channel, we heard Hamit's statements and intentions. However, Art and I heard something, a small thing the others didn't notice, something they <u>couldn't</u> notice. Hamit said he was 'about to blow thousands of infidels to hell, ricky-tick.' That unique phrase—'ricky tick'—and the somewhat familiar voice told us that 'Hamit' was actually Dan Stinson, the ungrateful jerk we hosted for a Bay tour.

"Instinctively, we hauled ass for Pier 39. Using his handheld radio, Art got on the designated frequency for our little group of Auxiliary vessels. He told them to follow us to Pier 39, tie up, and bring ashore handheld VHS radios and bullhorns. Their job was to clear spectators from the crowded dockside shopping facility. Committed men and women that they were, none asked questions; they moved into action immediately.

"We got there first and docked. I grabbed the handheld VHF and my bullhorn, then the three of us stepped onto the Pier 39 dock. We shoved our way to the waterside edge of the tourist center. Art and Steve used the bullhorn and their bodies to push the crowd back while I made radio contact with Hamit—actually Daniel Stinson— on the tanker. I confronted him using his Christian name. I said that the whole Islamic thing was a charade, that he was just a loser with an empty, miserable life."

The spectators at the Lions Club were enthralled, but Jackson paused and affected a more whimsical tone. "Look, I didn't know what to say to the terrorist, although I didn't find Stinson personally intimidating. I was trying to buy time for Art and the other Auxies who were herding people to safety. My bravado was probably fueled by adrenaline. I told Stinson—I refused to call him Hamit—that his plan was gonna fail, that the crowd at Pier 39 was gone. It wasn't yet, but he didn't know that."

The Lions laughed at that comment. Jackson paused and smiled. Then he continued by answering an obvious question.

"What was the Coast Guard Sector Command doing all this time? Put bluntly, they were going apeshit. They wanted us volunteers to stand down—get the hell out of there—but they couldn't reach us. My ongoing conversation with Stinson tied up the primary channel for them to get involved. Command did, however, dispatch multiple armed assets including helicopters and patrol boats to the scene.

"On the tanker, Stinson started to panic. I could hear it in his voice. Sometimes after he talked to me, I could hear him shouting and arguing with his two fellow thugs before releasing the press-to-talk lever on his microphone. They were imploring him to surrender. When Stinson refused, they jumped overboard.

"Talking again to me and believing that Pier 39 had been evacuated, Stinson mentioned other potential high-value targets nearby. I debunked each of them with truckloads of bullshit. Finally, Stinson said he would ram the boat <u>somewhere</u>, maybe Alcatraz, to cause an epic oil spill. Again, he held the PTT lever open.

"I started to worry. We had no way to stop that. Before I could think of a response, I heard a gunshot over the ship's radio. Then there was radio silence for a minute or so. Finally, the high-pitched voice of another passenger aboard *Gemini* said, 'Hamit or Daniel, whoever he was, is dead.'

"At the dock, we were too shocked to react, but someone at Coast Guard Sector San Francisco got on frequency and said, 'Vessel *Gemini*, say again your last, over.'

"The response was, 'This is Colin Hennessey, *a Gemini* passenger. I just shot your hijacker in the back of the head. I'm afraid it made quite a mess on the GPS.'"

The Lions chuckled and released their tension. Jackson noticed it was time to wrap up.

"Hennessey, the shooter, was one of *Gemini's* other passengers. He was a small and somewhat meek fellow, an introverted writer who often traveled aboard tankers and cargo ships. He carried a gun because of some traumatic events during his travels.

"The ship, now a crime scene, was taken over by the Coasties. The two hijackers in the water were picked up and arrested. The civilians and crew aboard the ship were questioned by the San Francisco Police Department. Each of us Auxiliarists at Pier 39 were debriefed by the Coast Guard's Sector JAG Officer. The Sector Commander stopped in to chew our asses, but then to congratulate us. He departed with a salute, and he spoke the Coast Guard's motto: 'Semper Paratus—Always Ready.'

"It was early morning when I made it home. The press was waiting at my house. They were like hungry jackals. My wife, Sharon, was traumatized by the day's events; she had watched a lot of it on live television. She was relieved when I got home, and she did her best to keep the press at bay. I made a statement, then I had a beer and went to sleep. It had been a long, eventful day, and I was pretty damned tired.

"And that's the story about the terrorist tanker in San Francisco. Thank you for your attention. I think we have time for a couple questions, right Tom?"

The audience applauded enthusiastically. Tom, the host, joined Jackson at the podium and thanked him for his heroism and his "thrilling tale." He thanked Art as well. Tom requested another round of applause, and the Lions responded with vigor.

Before the clapping subsided, a woman stood and asked, "Mr. Boyd, if that had all gone sideways, as a civilian-volunteer, what would they have done to you?"

Jackson said, "Assuming I survived, the Coast Guard couldn't court marshall me, so I guess I would have been prosecuted in criminal court, reckless endangerment or something like that. Put another way: I'd still be in prison instead of chatting with you folks tonight."

That brought another laugh from the crowd. Six hands shot up to indicate more questions. Before Jackson could receive a question, a deep, disembodied voice from the back of the room commented.

"You people are missing the point. Here's the message from that whole situation in San Francisco: we let too many dangerous foreigners into this country all————the————time, like those assholes you dealt with from the Middle East. Around here, it's the damned Cubans."

Tom froze. Audience heads swiveled to get a look at the crude, heavy-set man in the back. By then, Jackson was hungry and exhausted, so he wasn't in the mood for any bullshit. Even so, his first response was measured.

"I stated that those were <u>Americans</u> who took on Islamic names and raised hell aboard the *Gemini*. I'll add that Cuban immigrants are merely fleeing an oppressive government, a tough situation. They just want freedom like the rest of us. Heck, except for Native Americans, <u>all</u> our families came from somewhere else to enjoy freedom and opportunity in this country."

The Lions were on Jackson's side, but the short, middle-aged antagonist in the baggy yellow shorts continued.

"Why don't you take that attitude back to California? So many foreigners, I hear your ballots are in sixteen different languages, including goddam Arabic, Russian, and Farsa or whatever they speak in I-ran. How stupid is that? Arabs are killin' our soldiers overseas, and the Russians want to nuke us. They're our fuggin' enemies."

Big Art, though not a man easily intimidated, could see this was going down a rathole. Under his breath he said, "Jackson, let it go, and let's get outta here."

Jackson's blood pressure elevated; he lost his temper and ignored Art's suggestion. "You are ignorant, pal," he said. "This topic is far more complex than that."

The chubby man's face turned as red as his soiled crimson t-shirt. He stood and stepped forward aggressively, and in a raised voice he asked, "Did you just call me stupid?"

The room erupted. Lions moved to restrain the loudmouth, while Jackson stood his ground and nodded defiantly. Tom, the now-shaken moderator, attempted to calm the group. The best he could do, however, was to announce that the event was over and that the bar was closed.

The outraged, vocal audience slowly filed out of the building. Some came forward and shook hands with Jackson and Art. They apologized on behalf of the club for "the asshole in the back." On his way out, that same asshole gave Jackson a long, fierce look.

Jackson turned to Tom and asked him for details about the disruptive guy. Tom was frustrated; this was his show.

"I am <u>so</u> sorry and <u>so</u> embarrassed that happened," said Tom in an exasperated tone. "That was Ed Melnik. He's not a member. He runs a decent boat detailing operation called TN Detail Services. Personally, I think he is <u>big</u> trouble."

"Well, he's gone now," said Jackson, "and I don't expect to see him again. Good night, Tom."

"Good night, Jackson. Your talk was outstanding. Thank you so much."

CHAPTER FOUR

Jackson and Art awoke to a picture-postcard morning in the Keys. They both left the air conditioned house to be outside on the upper deck. They sat and stretched on ivory-white steel chairs with comfortable navy blue cushions; a ceiling fan whirled above them. At 10:00 AM, it was already warm and muggy.

"Is it always like this?" asked Jackson.

"Yeah, pretty much," said Art. "Summers are hotter. Winters can get chilly. The fall, especially September and early October, can be pretty rainy and windy; storms come up from the Caribbean. We might still see a bit of that this week given it is mid-October."

"It's a boater's paradise. No wonder you love it here."

"Correcto," said Art, "except for the occasional idiot like that guy last night. Hey, I was proud of how you stood up to him, Jackie."

"Yeah, this former purchasing manager is dauntless when he has a six-foot, five-inch warrior at his side."

"Hey, you did your time blasting off mortars in the Army. You can handle yourself."

Art changed the subject. "One of the things I like about the Keys, besides the spectacular waters," he said, "are the friendly people. The merchants are helpful, restaurant servers are nice; heck I find myself chatting with strangers all the time. You know that's not like me." Jackson nodded with understanding as he pushed his cereal around in the bowl.

"I see you went light there, Jackie. How's your stomach today?"

Jackson said, "Not great, but considering those gut bombs we ate from the gas station and the dust-up at the Lions Club, I am glad I'm not in the ER."

"Me too." After a pause, Art added, "Let's talk about today. The list of choices is long. Wanna hear it?"

"Sure, but how about the Cliff Notes version?"

Art listed his favorites, "Boating and a dockside lunch, dive museum, alligator farm, skydiving, Worldwide Sportsman—a huge store loaded with boat gear and boat clothing—a drive down the Keys to get the lay of the land, West Marine, an overpriced boat gear store like the ones in California."

He continued, "I can also introduce you to Hugo Vihlen, a sailing record holder and very good guy. Then there's Robert is Here, a giant fruit stand with unbeatable milkshakes."

"Wow. I'd better extend my stay another week," Jackson joked.

Art pointed to the bay and said, "We have a perfect day out there. Let's get the boat wet and go for some real Keys food."

"Sounds good. When do we leave?"

Art looked at his watch. "It's 10:30 now. How about we target an 11:15 departure? We're gonna go to the funkiest place in the Upper Keys. It's about forty minutes from here."

"Perfect," said Jackson.

"First a quick orientation." Art opened a nautical chart and spread it on the table. "We can and we <u>will</u> boat on both sides of Key Largo this week, the bay side and the ocean side. By the way, on land Highway 1, the road we came in on and runs the length of the Keys, is the official dividing line for bay side and ocean side. The bay side is where we are now. The seas here are calmer, and many of the routes we will use are part of the Intercoastal Waterway, at least a lot of us call it that. It is actually the InTRAcoastal Waterway.

"It starts around Boston and it runs for 3,000 miles along the Atlantic Seaboard and around Florida. Then it follows the Gulf of Mexico coast all the way to Brownsville, Texas."

Jackson was confused. "So, it runs inland that whole way? How can that be?"

"Good question. It's a waterway made up of inlets, bays, sounds, rivers and canals. You probably saw some markers in the distance when you stood on the dock yesterday. Those show the section of the ICW that runs through here." Jackson shook his head in amazement.

Art continued as he pointed out specifics on the chart. "Today, we'll stay on the bay side going through a series of cuts and sounds. The other side of the Keys is the ocean side. It is formally the Florida Straits, a patch of water flowing eastward from the Gulf of Mexico to the Atlantic. Cuba is located on the other side of the straits about 190 miles from here; it's 90 miles from Key West."

"This is great. Thanks Art. I'm lovin' this."

They showered and dressed. Jackson disliked sunscreen because it always felt like Pennzoil. That explained his ongoing problems with skin cancer; his forehead looked like the lunar surface. Nevertheless, he lathered his face and forehead.

"Hey Art," Jackson shouted from his bedroom, "you want some of this sunscreen? I finally found some Neutragena stuff that doesn't feel like 30-weight."

"No thanks. I am already basted like a turkey." They met up in the living room.

Art said, "I turned on power to the boatlift. Half the time I get down to the boat and I have forgotten to flip on the breaker in the hallway by your bedroom. Getting old sucks."

Art grabbed a green-striped canvas bag off the counter. He said, "Okay, I packed this stuff to take on the boat: chart, towel, bottled water, some granola bars, my cell phone, wallet, and a handheld VHF radio. I think that is everything."

His downward stare while speaking revealed he was working through a mental checklist. He reached into a basket near the front door and added, "Oh yeah, the boat key would help."

Jackson tossed his wallet and phone into the sun-bleached bag. Art mentioned it was a freebie from West Marine after he spent bundles there on lines, life jackets and other boating gear.

Art continued, "Okay. Let's go down to the boat room and gather lines, finders, life vests, and other stuff for the boat."

"Lead the way," said Jackson. "Do you lock your front door?"

"Yeah. A lot of folks here don't but I do. Not sure why. Being from California, maybe I'm less trusting than Keys folks."

The "boat room" below the main level was originally built as an added guest room. Officially, however, it could not serve as any form of living space per county regulations, because its elevation was within the floodplain. It was a convenient place to store boating gear. The room had its own air conditioning unit; with Florida being so humid, battling mildew was a constant chore.

Finally, they schlepped all the gear across the backyard field of scalding pea rock to the dock. Art knew it would take a few days to adjust to both the heat and humidity. He was wondering how Jackson was feeling, but he didn't ask. When boating, they always focused on hydration anyway.

As before, *Jenny Girl* sat gleaming high above the water on its electric lift. The lift operated something like a car mechanic's hoist where pressure points were placed beneath the car's undercarriage to raise it safely. For the boat lift, the points of contact were created by two long, heavy, carpet-covered boards, or bunks, that ran longitudinally under the boat. Unlike the mechanic's hoist, the boat lift's power hardware was mounted above the deck on four vertical pilings; they supported the structure that held electric powered rolling steel tubes and cables that were attached to the bunks. Depending on the direction the control levers were activated, the cables coiled or uncoiled to raise or lower the bunks and thus raise or lower the boat.

Art moved the two levers on a support post, and the boat lowered slowly. He shut off the lift when the boat was in the water but not yet afloat. That enabled them to board the boat without it rocking in the water. They loaded the gear and climbed aboard.

Jenny Girl was twenty-two feet long; it was built by Sailfish, an above-average brand in terms of quality. It had an open bow for seating and a fabric t-top to provide shade for the skipper and a passenger sitting with him at the helm. Art had upgraded the standard Yamaha 150-horsepower engine to a 200-horse one. Because it was a modern four-stroke motor, it didn't sound or smell like a 1950s-era John Deere tractor.

Once they stowed everything and flipped on the boat's main power switch, Art lowered the engine's outdrive. He looked back to ensure it was well into the water. He checked that the throttle was in neutral, then he switched on the ignition. The motor started instantly.

"Atta baby," Art said. "Jackie, this engine sits unused for months at a time, but it always fires right up. The folks at Yamaha are geniuses."

Jackson agreed. "There are some other good engines out there, like Honda, but I think Yamaha makes the best."

Art directed Jackson to finish lowering the boat further by reaching out and briefly pivoting the two levers from the boat. In a few seconds the Sailfish was afloat. Art said, "Backing down," to announce he was shifting into reverse and advancing the throttle.

Per their regular practice, Jackson affirmed the action. "Backing down," he repeated.

They left Art's slip, turned 180 degrees and motored slowly for 300 yards. Jackson could see the seaweed on the bottom; the water was barely four feet deep. When the depth sounder read a depth of five feet and after signaling he was increasing power, Art advanced the throttle aggressively. The boat lurched forward and quickly picked up speed. In four or five seconds, the boat was on plane and hustling north at thirty miles per hour—26 knots—across Buttonwood Sound.

The engine noise was moderate; they could chat comfortably. Jackson commented, "Very nice. Those 200 horses push this thing easily. What a nice ride." The wind was calm, and the water was flat.

Art nodded. He pointed to the color GPS screen and described their intended course. "See this cut just ahead? That's gonna take us through the mangroves to Tarpon Basin, then through another cut and so on, just like I showed you on the chart."

CHAPTER FIVE

The ride was smooth over the twenty-seven miles to Alabama Jack's. Jackson drove the boat about half the time. Just before the Card Sound Bridge, Art took the boat down a canal. Because of often present manatees, he slowed the boat to idle speed, about four miles per hour. A few minutes later they were approaching the restaurant.

"Is that it ahead on the right?" asked Jackson.

"Yup," said Art. "We will pass it slowly, do a 180 then dock on the port side. Would you please ready the lines and fenders?"

"Got it skipper."

As they passed the restaurant, patrons sitting along the rail responded. Some pointed, some gave a thumbs up. The boat's unique name got a lot of favorable attention in South Florida. Art spun the boat and made a perfect approach to the dock, shifting to neutral at just the right time. Jackson stepped off and secured the bow line to a dock cleat. Art put the throttle into neutral, then he stepped off the boat to secure the stern line. With the boat tied down, he climbed back aboard and shut down the engine. Jackson and Art grabbed their wallets and the boat key before walking up the dock to the entrance of the open air restaurant.

Upon entering, Art waved and shouted, "Hi Mike" to the smiling, fortyish man with a crew cut behind the bar. Despite the heat he was wearing a hockey sweater.

"Hey Art," Mike responded, "grab a seat anywhere."

Art commented to Jackson, "Great guy and a hard worker. His family has owned this place forever. They have another place in Ohio maybe, on one of the Great Lakes."

They took a table in the shade. The temperature was in the high eighties, although the overhead fans helped against the heat. A server stopped by with menus and asked about drinks.

"I'd like a Bud Light, please," said Art. Jackson ordered the same.

Jackson looked around. The view of the canal was pleasant and it offered a breeze. Trees lined the canal's swampy-looking far side. The chairs and tables inside the place were basic. A vertically mounted wooden dowel held a paper towel roll at each table; those were the napkins. Colorful license plates from seemingly everywhere lined the beams above. Strings of crab pot markers—colored styrofoam balls smaller than volleyballs—hung from the ceiling. Art described the decor as "Keys chic."

In the back and off to one side, there was an empty ten-foot by ten-foot elevated bandstand made of unfinished pine. An absence of tables near the bandstand created a dance floor on the restaurant's basic concrete surface. A door from a vintage airplane hung near the bandstand; a red ball and the caricature of a bathing beauty had been painted on it many decades earlier. Nearby, there were wire coat hangers displaying a variety of long sleeve souvenir t-shirts.

As the beers arrived, Jackson said, "This is great, perfect." Then he asked Art, "What do you recommend we eat?"

"I like the smoked fish pieces and the conch fritters. Okay with you if we get an order of each?"

"Just what is 'conch'?" Jackson asked.

"Oh, sorry. It's pronounced 'konk.' The conch shell is the one you sometimes see people blowing at sunset in, say, Hawaii. It sounds a bit like a high-pitched foghorn. The part you eat is the animal inside. It's like a muscle. Think of small fried bits sorta like abalone."

"Got it. Yeah, that works for me."

Jackson raised his beer and said, "Here's to a fun week in paradise. Thanks for bringing me here." They clinked bottles and they each took a hearty pull of the Bud.

After they ordered, Art said, "Jackie, last night I was impressed with your passion about immigration. I'd like to chat about that a bit. Okay with you?"

"Yeah, sure. Do you have a reaction to anything I said?"

"Not specifically," said Art. "We have never talked about it, but from your comments I suspect I am more conservative than you."

"How so?"

"The Cubans fleeing an oppressive government. I got the impression you supported open borders," said Art.

"I just don't think we should build walls, if that's what you mean," Jackson stated.

"No walls, no gates: those are, by definition, open borders. So anyone can just walk or swim across and live in the U.S.?" Then Art said, "Wait, wait. Before you answer that question, Jackie, I have a joke for you. It goes back a ways, but it is funny." Art chuckled to himself, then he continued.

"Why didn't Mexico send a team to the 1980 Olympic Games in Los Angeles?" Jackson shrugged. "Because everyone who could run, jump or swim was already there." Jackson chuckled.

Then Art asked, "Oops, is that a racist joke or an exaggerated social observation? It is not <u>disparaging</u> of Latinos; it is only noting that there are many Mexican immigrants in that area. L.A. is nearly fifty percent Latino now."

"I don't have an issue with the joke," said Jackson, "and we both know Mexico <u>did</u> send a team to L.A. in 1980. But your reference to 'open borders' is not accurate. We do have checkpoints at the main crossing points. It's not <u>that</u> simple."

"But we aren't really talking about the *ease* of crossing the frontier. We both know that plenty of people avoid the checkpoints and simply come across, not to say it's an easy journey. The Border Patrol can't keep up with the volume; folks who get caught come back again. It is like a stupid, expensive game," said Art.

"It's hardly a game. Most of those people are risking their lives and abandoning everything familiar to them. As I said last night, they are simply seeking the same freedom you and I enjoy."

The food arrived. The two men continued the conversation while they ate. Fortunately, neither was getting worked up. That spoke to their mutual respect.

Art continued. "I get all that, but how do we assimilate people in numbers we have no control over? How do <u>they</u> assimilate without language skills and the legal right to work? To me, that adds up to their living below the radar, an 'underclass' of people forming communities, ghettos, with other illegals. Whoops I said the 'I-word'. I've noticed that pro-immigration people now call them 'Dreamers.' For me that packages their views in favorable cosmetics."

"They <u>do</u> have dreams. They dream to have a better life for themselves and their families. As I said last night, our ancestors all came from outside the United States. Their dreams motivated them to make the needed sacrifices to get here. How is that different from, say, the Cubans? Their situation is shit."

"True that," said Art. "I just think we should know who is entering the country if only for security reasons. It could be that as a career military and law enforcement guy, I prefer order and control. To me the immigration situation seems to be without rational processes; it's chaos."

Jackson said, "We all see this through our own lens and our own experiences. For sure it's complicated."

The server removed their paper plates, and she asked about dessert.

"Jackie, some Key Lime Pie?"

"None for me. I'm full." Art asked for the check.

"On me, big guy. That was our deal," Jackson said. Art nodded.

Jackson paid the check and they returned to the boat. Art fired her up, and Jackson released the lines and climbed aboard. As Art pulled off the dock, Jackson stowed the lines and fenders.

"The wind has kicked up," said Jackson.

"Yeah, that is typical for the afternoon. Fortunately it is behind us and the chop isn't bad." The small talk was limited. Neither was mad; each was just mulling their lunch conversation.

Art put the boat into his home slip with ease. Jackson temporarily secured the boat with a line around a dock post. On Art's command, Jackson reached up to turn the levers that lifted the boat enough to hold the vessel, temporarily and not rocking in the water, at a good height for finishing up. Art used a switch on the boat engine to forward rotate the motor and propeller high and out of the water.

They put their personal gear on the deck. Jackson took it inside while Art dealt with the engine. He flushed the saltwater from the motor's cooling jacket by unscrewing a plastic fitting on the cowling and connecting it to a dockside hose. While the fresh water flowed through the engine, Art sat in the shade for about fifteen minutes. Then he removed the hose and reconnected the fitting to the engine. He climbed off the boat gond raised the lift to its original, high position.

Back in the house, they each grabbed a Kalik and lounged on the upper deck. As the northern breeze flowed over them, their conversation drifted to logistics. They needed groceries, but neither wanted to leave the deck.

"Art," said Jackson, "how about I go to the store for some food?"

"That's nice of you. Are you feeling up to it?"

"Not really. Between the jetlag and my howling gut, I'd be happy to sit right here until tomorrow. But it needs to get done, and you were on tour guide duty all day."

"You are a trooper, Jackie," said Art. "I have a solution: Domino's is five minutes from here."

"Perfect. I'll buy if you fly," replied Jackson, though he wasn't sure if pizza was the best remedy for an upset stomach.

They negotiated which pizza to get. First was the size. Art could eat a giant pizza by himself. Given the state of his stomach, Jackson only wanted a slice or two. Next came the ingredients. Art was a combo guy; he would eat pizzas with a lamb chop if they made them. Jackson was a purist—cheese and pepperoni only. As they often did, they compromised and ordered a large pizza, half pepperoni, half junkyard dog. Art would be glad to eat any leftover pepperoni.

Art fetched the pizzas, and they ate like hounds. The boat's constant motion and the fresh salty air always made the both men very hungry. After eating, Art checked the weather forecast for Tuesday. It was going to be very windy so they resolved to sleep in. Art also suggested lunch at his favorite place.

They watched junk television on Art's huge living room screen for the rest of the evening until they both nodded off on the sofas. They woke up at half-past midnight to the Cheers theme song. Without comment they snapped off the lights and shuffled to their bedrooms.

CHAPTER SIX

El Melnik spoke into his scuffed Samsung phone. "Hey Tina, it's dad."

"Oh hi dad, thanks for calling." Tina's voice sounded raspy.

"Well sure, hun. I've been thinking about your sore throat, and I wanted to see if you got the test results back."

"Yeah," Tina responded, "it was strep' after all. Doctor Wiersig has me on antibiotics, and I am taking Advil for the throat pain. Feeling a lot better today."

"I'm relieved to hear that, hon. Keep gettin' lots of rest though, right?"

"Sure. Work can wait, and I have plenty of sick leave. How are you doing, dad?"

"I'm on a job right now, waxing up a 24-foot Grady-White in the customer's carport," said Ed. "Jerry and I are takin' a break. Only one other job is scheduled this week, Friday. October is never a great month. Snowbirds aren't here yet, and the locals worry about hurricanes though there's nothin' on the radar. It all evens out, I guess."

Tina asked, "Are you still glad you bought that business after mom died? It's been about four years now, and we still miss you in Fort Myers."

"Oh yeah. I did the right thing, and I needed a change. Things are good, though it's different down here…" Ed's voice trailed off.

"Different how? Keys people seem like nice folks, but it probably gets old dealing with the tourists."

"I guess," said Ed. "To be honest, my bids keep gettin' undercut by most detailing services in town. They hire illegals and they pay 'em squat. It's unfair, and it pisses me off."

Ed's "dad-voice" had gotten louder. Ed's coworker, Pablo, overheard the reference to illegals. He looked up from his *Velveeta* sandwich and nodded agreement. Pablo was of Cuban descent, but his family had gone through the formal immigration process and he had a green card.

"Why can't <u>you</u> do that, dad?" Tina asked. Then she added, "No offense to you Pablo, if you can hear me."

Ed's voice lost all its softness. He said, "I won't do that! There are plenty of Americans needing jobs. I'll go outta business before hiring illegals. The foreigners are killin' our economy."

Tina was sympathetic, but she knew to truncate the conversation about "foreigners." Though her dad's frustration was legitimate and understandable, a champion debater couldn't offer enough logic to change his views. If Ed had a hot button, this was it.

"Well dad," she said, "You are a good dad, you work hard, and you are a man of conviction. I have always loved you for all that."

"Thanks. I'd better get back to work. I'm <u>so</u> glad you're feeling better, but keep takin' it easy."

"I will. I love you, dad."

"Love you, too, hun."

After Tina ended the call, she wondered, for the 800th time, how her dad would react if he knew she was bisexual. With his views being so attached to the past, that was a conversation she <u>never</u> wanted to have.

At the end of the day, Ed returned to his home in Key Largo on Abaco Road. He lived on the ocean side of Highway 1, near the intersection where Highway 905 breaks off and heads north to the posh, gated Ocean Reef Club private resort. His place was a two bedroom, one bath cinder block house with a red tin roof that was more rusted than red. The aluminum window frames were in disrepair. A dripping air conditioning unit sagged from a side window with a board to cover the missing glass.

Ed parked his red Chevy truck along the street. His tired, nineteen-foot skiff and trailer occupied the driveway. He was soaked with perspiration; he had worked hard, and the 196 pounds on his broad, five-foot, nine-inch frame were especially burdensome. A bright point of his day besides chatting with Tina: Ed had been paid in cash. That transaction would never appear on the books of his company, TN Detail Services. Although it sounded like a business in Tennessee, Ed kept the company's name when he bought it. He wanted to avoid confusion among the public and within TN's legacy customer base.

Inside the house, Ed pulled a can of Amstel Light from the fridge. He collapsed into his cracked, brown leather lounger and turned on the television. It was after 6:00 PM, so Special Report with Brett Baier was airing live on channel seven, Fox News. That was the last channel he watched after the Lions Club event the previous night.

On Fox News, he liked checking out Martha MacCallum between 7 PM and 8 PM. Ed thought she was smart and smoking hot. For commentary and interviews, his favorite was Tucker Carlson Tonight at 8 PM. Of course, Carlson was a conservative like Ed, but Carlson also brought on guests with whom he disagreed. Ed liked the sparring, and he sometimes agreed with the guests.

For balance, Ed sometimes watched CNN. The only host he could stand was Anderson Cooper despite Cooper being openly gay. He considered the others on CNN to be sensationalistic hacks. Ironically, Cooper appeared during the same time slot as Tucker Carlson. In his heart, however, Ed knew they were <u>all</u> partisans, including Carlson, spinning opinion and dogma into so-called news.

Just as Martha McCallum was coming on Fox, Ed's cell phone rang. His ringtone was a repeating snippet of the Beach Boys' song, "Kokomo." That tune always gave him a chuckle; contrary to the song's lyrics, there is no place called Kokomo in the Florida Keys. Ed muted the TV and checked the caller ID. It was his fishing buddy, Lenny Dunbar.

"Yo, Lenny. How ya doin?"

"Hi Ed, I am just swell, thanks for asking," Lenny replied. Lenny was a retired, sixty-seven year-old bookkeeper from Dayton, Ohio.

Ed was tickled by Lenny's choice of words. "Swell" was a long-dead adjective still in use only by elderly folks from the upper Midwest. He responded, "We're due for a day of fishin' and tellin' lies, aren't we Lenny?"

This was Ed's way of inviting himself aboard Lenny's boat. He preferred riding Lenny's comfortable, tricked-out 22-foot Mako. Its 200-horse' Yamaha four-stroke motor was powerful yet quiet, and its black Bimini top provided much-needed shade out on the water.

"Yes, Ed, that's why I called. Helen is in full shrew mode. Have any time this week, any day but Thursday?"

"Tomorrow and Wednesday are out. So is Friday; I have a customer that morning. How 'bout Saturday?"

"It'll have to be Saturday, I guess. Okay if we take my boat?"

Score. "Sure, Lenny. You're the fisher-king. Whatever works best for you."

"Okay. Let's plan for Saturday."

Lenny paused and then asked, "Hey Ed, can you please meet up for lunch sometime sooner? I gotta get out of the house and away from She-Devil."

"Okay. I'll move some things around. I'll make tomorrow work." Ed was chuckling, because he knew Helen was indeed a pain to be around.

"Ed, you're a savior. I'll see you at the usual place, one o'clock."

"Got it, Lenny. See you then. Bye."

After the call, Ed retrieved another Amstel Light and settled to watch Martha MacCallum just being pretty. He didn't bother to un-mute the television. Forty minutes later, he fell asleep just before Carlson and Cooper came on.

CHAPTER SEVEN

Tuesday morning, Ed had errands to run. He delivered more tax documents to his CPA. His federal taxes were overdue, and one last batch of contrived scribbles gave his accountant enough data to complete his return. Next, Ed got one of his truck tires fixed. After two weeks, he had become weary of stopping for air every other day. Finally, just before his lunch with Lenny, he stopped at CVS drugstore to pick up toilet paper, beef jerky, his Eliquis blood-thinner prescription and a twelve-pack of Amstel Light.

Lenny and Ed both arrived at Mrs. Mac's restaurant at 1 PM. As they entered, Lenny thanked Ed for meeting him, and Lenny demanded that he be allowed to treat Ed to lunch. Ed shrugged and nodded agreement. Just inside the door, the hostess welcomed the men and told them to sit anywhere. Ed scanned the room and spotted an empty table for two next to the Californians from the Lions Club gathering. He said to Lenny, "Follow me." They slid past the bar and were soon seated.

When Art noticed Ed nearby, he mumbled, "Ohhhh shiiiit." Puzzled, Jackson looked up from his Coconut Shrimp Plate, then he too saw Ed. Neither of them recognized the thin, gray, bookish man accompanying Ed.

Jackson said nothing, and he returned his attention to his lunch. Art did the same. But Ed greeted them both.

"Hi guys. Why aren't you maritime legends out on the water?" he asked.

Without looking, Jackson said, "Too windy."

"What?! You Coast Guard weenies are put off by a little chop? I've heard San Fran' Bay is rough, but based on the fantasy I heard Sunday night, I assumed you two were ironmen. I guess not."

This time it was Art's turn to put Ed in his place.

"Look Ed—that's your name, right? Look Ed, just eat your lunch and shut your big mouth," he said. When Jackson snickered at Art's comment, he accidentally spit bits of food.

Art was confused. He said to Jackson, "What?"

"Art, how's Eddie-the-Bigot here supposed to eat while he keeps his mouth shut? Are you guys related?"

Art laughed, but Ed was pissed. Lenny was simply confused by all the insults; however Ed was not in a mood to explain.

He said to Art, "So, you two California fags out lookin' for some sweet young Cuban boys today? I think I saw some pullin' weeds at Founders Park. Ya might wanna hustle down there."

Art rolled his eyes and said, "Recess is over, little Eddie. Don't you need to get back to your classroom at Racist Elementary?"

Jackson jumped in, addressing Ed directly. "Shitbird, Sunday night you said 'We let too many dangerous foreigners into this country.' After you left the Lions Club, Tom told us your name is Melnik, Ed Melnik, right? I checked with Mr. Google, and he said that Melnik is a Russian and Jewish name, and that is just fine. For a guy who is pretty 'ethnic' himself you sure talk a lot of shit about others."

Ed was livid; he stood up. Then, in slow motion, he patted his untucked, flowered shirt at his right hip where a concealed weapon might be carried. He spoke to Jackson through gritted teeth.

"I'll be seein' you again, soon, and it won't be in a crowded bar like this." Then he darted for the door.

Lenny was still puzzled. To no one in particular, he asked, "What the hell just happened?"

Art responded. "Ed and my friend Jackson here exchanged unpleasantries Sunday night at the Lions Club. This was round two. Let's all hope there is no round three."

Lenny looked at Jackson; then, he looked at the floor. Without saying anything more, he shook his head and left the restaurant.

CHAPTER EIGHT

"Well, Jackie," said Art, "I think you have a new fan in Mr. Ed, although the word 'stalker' comes to mind."

"Lucky me," said Jackson. His mouth was partially full. Then he changed the subject. "You were right about this Key Lime Pie. I haven't made the rounds here yet, but this is fantastic."

"My favorite for sure," said Art. "Let's make it a challenge to check out the other candidates. Can you live with that?"

"Key Lime Pie every day? Twist my arm, although Sharon won't recognize me next week."

Jackson and Art exited Mrs. Mac's. Outside in the blazing Florida sun, Art said, "It's yet another gorgeous day in the Keys. What are you up for?"

"Hmmm. You mentioned some amazing stuff yesterday. The idea of skydiving got my attention, and the breeze has laid down. I checked out the Skydive Miami website, and it looked like fun. Do we have time to do that?"

"Atta boy Jackie. Let's do it. I'll call to be sure they're still flying in the afternoon. They're in Homestead, not Miami. It'll take about forty-five minutes to get there. They're sorta near your new favorite gas station-slash-gourmet eatery, RaceTrac."

Art confirmed by phone that jumps would be offered until sunset. They had time. Without stopping at the house to change clothes, they drove Highway 1 back up the stretch and into Florida City, just past RaceTrac to the main intersection. Art made a left turn on West Palm Drive. They were heading into the sticks. After just over a mile, they stopped at a rural but busy intersection. There, Jackson got his first look at Robert is Here, the enormous fruit stand, zoo, shake shop and museum Art mentioned on Sunday.

"Wow," said Jackson. "You said this was a big deal, but I didn't imagine this. Why is there a line of people that extends into the parking lot?"

"They are waiting either to order or pick up their milkshakes. As I told you yesterday, they have the best shakes ever, like twenty different kinds. I think we need to stop here after testing gravity. Yes?"

"Sure. If I survive, I will have earned it. Calories-be-damned when your life is at stake. On that note, the skydive website said they had a weight limit of 240 pounds. It's a good thing we are doing this early in the week."

They drove past Robert's, made a right turn, and soon they arrived at the Miami Homestead General Aviation Airport—a rather grand name for a 4,000-foot airstrip of asphalt situated on Florida scrubland. Skydive Miami sat to the left of the runway on a long patch of parched grass. There was no sizable skydive airplane in sight, just a few other squat buildings, a couple of small Cessnas, and a Mooney.

The Californians parked and approached the wide cinder block building. Men and women wearing harnesses waited at green colored picnic tables for their jump times. Family members and sweethearts were seated with them. No one looked more than thirty years old.

Jackson and Ed entered the building and approached the counter. Framed photos of in-air jumpers covered the light blue walls. There were also counters with wooden stools, a water cooler, and at the end of the spacious room, there were glass cases with souvenir t-shirts. Jackson was impressed; the place looked very professional.

"How can I help you gentlemen?" asked a smiling, tanned, twenty-something man with a blond ponytail. He looked like the prototypical California surfer.

Art said, "My buddy here wants to fall from the sky. Got a tandem slot left?"

"Two slots, actually," clarified Jackson.

Before young Adonis could respond, Art said, "Oh no, Jackie. I'm not doin' that." His voice was firm.

There was a long pause. The counter attendant waited for his two customers to sort things out. They stepped to the side and had a conversation using soft voices.

Jackson said, "Art, you're a former Ranger. This is a piece 'a cake for you. I'm happy to pay for your jump. I'd planned to anyway."

"I had to make three jumps to get my Ranger tab. I hated it, and I was glad I never had to jump again. Nope. I'll watch."

"I don't understand," said Jackson. "What about all that stuff in Vietnam? You didn't jump then?"

"Nope. We inserted in the bush by rappelling from hovering helicopters. It was faster and safer. If we'd used 'chutes, we'd have been dangling targets for the NVA."

Jackson edged toward the counter and said to the attendant, "So, it's just me."

The attendant nodded and said, "Sir, we have a ride for you in an hour and fifteen minutes. Okay?"

Jackson nodded. His mind was still processing Art's comments.

"Good," said surf-man. "In the meantime, we will get you signed up. After some paperwork, you will watch a safety video, and you will receive some personal instruction from your experienced tandem partner. Do you want photos or a video of your jump?"

"No thanks."

Though not panicking, Jackson realized this was getting real. As he had learned to do during some shitty days in the Army, Jackson shut off the analytical part of his brain, wherever that was. He resolved to listen, follow instructions, roll out of the plane, and try to enjoy the ride down. His stomach was also reacting, not in a good way, to the rich Key Lime Pie. He resolved to visit the mens room before getting on the plane.

From outside the shack, they heard the sound of tires skidding and the roar of an aircraft engine. Jackson and Art stepped outside to see the single-engine jump plane finish its roll. Near the end of the runway, it turned and taxied in their direction. It looked new: white on the upper side, navy blue on the lower side. A longitudinal yellow stripe separated the other colors.

"Wuddya think Jackie?" asked Art.

"It looks spacious and airworthy, I guess. That's a big exit door on the right side. It must be windy as hell when they are flying." Art didn't respond. They returned to the counter to finish the details.

The attendant said, "Our bird is a late-model Cessna Caravan. It's made for this type of duty. Just the ride to altitude is a blast."

Jackson was starting to like the kid.

The young man continued. "You have a choice of experiences. You can jump from 8,000 feet, with a freefall of about twenty seconds. You can jump from 10,500 feet with a freefall of roughly forty seconds. I recommend our best value, the Extreme Tandem Jump from 13,500 feet. You'll have a spectacular view from the Keys all the way Miami Beach, and your freefall will last about a minute. Should I sign you up for that?"

This kid is selling. He's good. Jackson asked the young man's name.

"I'm Andy. Hi. And your name?"

"My name is Jackson Boyd. Nice to meet you, Andy. And yes, I'd like the full monty. What does that cost?"

Andy looked confused. It seemed that the "full monty" reference didn't resonate with him.

Jackson clarified his meaning. "Sorry. I'm thinking about the jump from 13,500 feet. What does it cost?"

"Oh. It's only $249.00. That includes the jump harness, soft-leather helmet, goggles, altimeter and complete training. Will you be paying by cash, check or charge?" *There he goes again, this time with a presumptive close. The kid will own this place in five years.*

"Charge," said Jackson, "I want my heirs to have a record of my foolishness." He was feeling good now.

"I guarantee you're gonna love it, Jackson. Please sign here."

Once that was taken care of, Jackson was asked to sign a lengthy legal release form. The word "dangerous" appeared at least ten times. After that, he watched a fifteen minute training video. "Death or serious injury" was mentioned another dozen times. *Does anyone ever survive these jumps?*

Eventually, Jackson was introduced to his instructor and tandem partner, Chris. Art excused himself to go outside for the duration and sit on a bench. Andy told Art how to reach the landing zone. It was very close by, a five-minute drive to an open field. Chris said Art could wait there for him and Jackson to "drop in." Art liked that idea. He planned to be standing by to congratulate his buddy.

As they walked to the yellow equipment room, Jackson asked Chris, "How many jumps have you made. No offense, but I have underwear older than you."

Chris laughed. "That's a fair question, Mr. Boyd. I am only twenty-three, but I have been doing this since I was eighteen. I earned my USPA certification when I was twenty. I have done over five hundred jumps, and I haven't so much as twisted an ankle. I also have my CPR certification."

"Yikes, I hope we won't be needing that," said Jackson.

"No, no CPR means Certified Parachute Rigger. I packed the 'chute we're gonna wear."

Chris paused a beat, thinking, then he asked Jackson, "Did you see Kurt Russell in the movie *Backdraft*?"

Jackson was confused, and he said, "Yeah why, are we jumping through fire today?"

"Nah. At the end of the movie in a burning warehouse, Russell's character, Bull, is straining to hold onto Scott Glenn's hand as the two dangle from a scaffold. Glenn looks up and says, 'Let me go, Bull.' There is a pause, then Russell says, 'Where you go, we go.' That's sorta the deal here."

"Well that just got dark," said Jackson. "Jesus, you sure took the fun outta this. Maybe I should consider juggling chainsaws today instead of skydiving."

"Sorry. I used our own mantra to let you know I'm seriously invested in your safety. I should have just said, 'I packed the parachute personally, so I am as invested in safety as much as you.' Was that better?"

"Ya think?! Whatever. Let's do this," said Jackson.

John Gordon

CHAPTER NINE

Chris confirmed that the Caravan would lift off well before the end of the runway. The plane would climb, then they would jump from 13,500 feet. Chris also said it would be "a little chilly" at altitude. He fitted Jackson with a harness, a pair of goggles, a soft, black, padded leather helmet, and a simple wristband altimeter. From the neck up, Jackson resembled Snoopy, the Peanuts cartoon character, ready to fight the Red Baron.

Jackson was told to lay on a bench, belly down. Chris put him into a "spread eagle" position with his chin up and his legs bent at the knees. Chris adjusted Jackson's arms to a mild forward bias.

"That is the position you will take when we're falling," said Chris.

Chris tapped Jackson on the back, and he stood up to face the instructor.

"As we fall out the door—we don't actually jump—I want your arms folded across your upper body like this." Chris demonstrated the position of the arms; Jackson mirrored him.

"Also as we leave the plane, I will toss a drone chute, a tiny parachute on a tether attached to my harness. It will create modest drag and keep us stable as we fall. We will freefall for about fifty seconds. Our speed will increase to our terminal velocity of about 125 miles per hour. It's really fun."

"Wait, wait," said Jackson, "terminal velocity? I don't like the sound of that. Just kidding: I know that is the fastest that physics will allow us to fall."

Chris continued. "At around 6,000 feet, I will pull the rip.' There will be a sudden jerk when it deploys. After that, we will drift nicely to our LZ. It will be very serene during that time. You'll hardly notice you are dropping; we'll even be able to chat."

"Quick question," said Jackson. By now the two men were on sarcasm terms. "This sturdy harness has a strap on each side going under my crotch. It is already tight. When this 'sudden jerk' happens, are my boys gonna be pushed up into my chest cavity?"

"Um, you will feel some pressure, but it's not <u>that</u> bad. You don't want any more kids anyway, do ya?"

Jackson chuckled and shook his head. Then Chris talked about the landing.

"From above, you will see a forty-foot circle of sand in a grassy field. That's our target, and I will guide us there by manipulating the shrouds. When we are pretty low, I will slow our descent significantly. Just above the ground, maybe twenty feet, I want you to extend your legs high in front of you, knees straight. That way, my legs will hit the ground first. After I touch down, you must quickly put your legs down. We may lunge forward a step or two, but we will remain upright. Make sense?"

Jackson was again sarcastic. "Darn. I was hoping for one of those behind-the-enemy-lines drop-and-roll routines. Then we gather the parachute and quickly bury it."

This time, Chris didn't get it, at all. *My God. Don't these kids ever watch old war movies?*

"Forget it. I was just being silly," Jackson said somewhat sheepishly. "This all sounds good to me. When do we go?"

"In a few minutes. A couple final details. On the plane I will become your human backpack. The whole time during the flight, we will be sitting and attached to each other, probably at the back of the plane. At altitude, you will see folks going out the door. As they do, we'll have to scooch on our butts toward the door. Okay? The noise will be extreme. Before it is our turn to go, I'll check your status with a thumbs-up. If you are good to go, give me a thumbs-up back."

"Got it. What if I am <u>not</u> good to go?"

"Well, you'll get to savor a short and expensive plane ride back to the airport," said Chris, "but I can see in your eyes that you've got this, Mr. Boyd."

"Thanks, but please call me Jackson. We're jumping out of a perfectly good airplane while you're humping my back; I'd like to think we're on familiar terms."

Chris smiled and nodded. Then he said it was time to go. It was over ninety degrees on the tarmac; Jackson was glad to be wearing just khaki cargo shorts and a yellow polo shirt. They walked toward the aircraft's right side. It's propeller was twirling at an idle pace.

Using a ladder, they climbed aboard. As Chris predicted, they sat in the back of the fuselage away from the large, square door. Chris secured Jackson's stainless carabiners to the adjacent loops on his own harness. Then he checked them again to ensure they were secure.

Five other "Siamese-jumpers" boarded and sat snugly in front of Jackson and Chris. Four colorfully dressed, laughing and joking solo-jumpers boarded last. They used the word "dude" a lot. They sat by the door. Clearly, they were very confident.

A crew member pulled down a sliding, clear plexiglass panel over the large doorway. With the plane buttoned up, it's engines revved. The aircraft taxied, barreled down the runway and lifted off. It took a surprisingly steep angle into the azure Florida sky. After a few minutes, it seemed to Jackson that they would soon level off to jump. He looked at his altimeter: 6,540 feet. *Oh man. We're gonna jump from twice this height? Maybe I should have bought the cheaper package.*

In another ten or fifteen minutes, the plane did level off. The crewman lifted the plex' door, and the wind rushed in. Jackson checked his altimeter: 13,528 feet. *Hey, I got an extra twenty-eight feet, free. Damn, it's getting cold.*

Without waiting for a signal, the dudes rolled out the door. The tandem jumpers scooched forward, getting nearer the door. Chris checked the carabiners once more. Jackson's heart raced, but not because of the impending tumble through space: he realized he had failed to visit the head before liftoff. The old meme, "Bring me my brown pants!" might in his case turn out to be legitimate.

Jackson and Chris were at the door. From behind, Chris helped Jackson fold his arms across his chest, then he lifted Jackson's chin and shoved them both off the airplane. They tumbled once, then they assumed the practiced drop position, arms and legs outstretched. As expected, the drone 'chute Chris deployed helped stabilize them.

It was cold, <u>freaking</u> cold—around fifty degrees. The temperature also reflected the piercing effects of falling at more than a hundred miles per hour. Jackson wondered why jumpsuits hadn't been offered. Worse, his face felt like it was freezing, literally.

They were in freefall for under a minute, though it seemed to Jackson like a lot longer. He looked at his unwinding altimeter: 8500, 8000, 7500, 7000. Soon after, Chris pulled the ripcord, and their descent slowed noticeably. Jackson's "boys" were fine, however.

With the 'chute fully deployed, the remainder of the fall was pleasant. As advertised, Jackson could see down the Keys and north to Miami. There were lush green fields, a meandering coastline, pods of multicolored neighborhoods and the stunning waters of South Florida.

"This is spectacular," he said over his shoulder, "no wonder you have a passion for this."

Chris replied, "Yeah, it is addicting. Maybe you should get certified. It isn't that hard."

"I take enough risks in my life. I don't need more."

Soon after, Jackson looked down and spotted a white circle. He asked, "Is that our landing spot?"

"That's it," said Chris. "I will make some turns as we approach." The approach happened quickly. Soon they were only fifty feet above ground.

Chris said, "Here we go. Get those feet out front."

The sandy circle came up to meet them. Chris' feet hit the ground, then Jackson's lowered his feet. If this was Olympic gymnastics, ABC's Al Michaels would have said they "stuck the landing."

To set him free, Chris unhooked Jackson's carabiners. Then Chris gathered the parachute and lines, and he accepted Jackson's harness and gear. There was no urgency to leave the sandpit: they were the last jumpers out of the plane.

"Great job," said Chris.

Jackson was very pleased. "It was all thanks to <u>you</u>. You are the consummate professional," he said. "You handled my sarcasm and bullshit very well. I had a lot of fun, and I felt safe. Oh, and I am glad you packed that 'chute correctly."

Jackson pulled out his wallet and handed Chris a fifty-dollar tip. Chris thanked Jackson, and the men shook hands. Jackson turned to walk off the sand. He saw Art coming toward him, smiling. Before greeting Art, Jackson spun around for a final word with Chris.

"Chris, before we left the aircraft, you didn't ask me for a thumbs up."

With faux confusion on his face and in his voice, Chris said, "Gee, I must have forgotten," then he turned and walked away.

Art approached Jackson and said, "Well Jackie, as they say after you first jump in Ranger School, 'You popped your cherry.' Congratulations." Art gave Jackson a bearhug.

Jackson felt very proud, and he said, "I have to admit, it was a lot of fun."

After saying that, Jackson felt a bit guilty. Parachuting had <u>not</u> been fun for Art in Ranger School, and Jackson did it with an expert strapped to his back. That was <u>very</u> different from bailing out solo.

Jackson kept his enthusiasm in check as they walked to the SUV. On the drive home, they made a quick bathroom stop for Jackson's relief. Back on the road, Art asked him a lot of questions about the skydiving experience. Jackson appreciated Art's interest, but he kept the details brief.

They decided not to stop for milkshakes at Robert is Here, though they resolved to come back another day. They still had no groceries at the house, so they stopped at Hobo's for dinner.

John Gordon

CHAPTER TEN

Just after sunrise a tired, small, pretty woman with long brown hair spoke. "Well, we made it through the first night, thankfully."

There were groans among the rain-soaked immigrants. Even their blankets were drenched. Luckily, their food and personal belongings stayed dry. The morning air was fouled with the smell of vomit. Some people stood on the rocking boat to stretch. A fresh morning breeze helped clear their lungs and fill the boat's filthy cotton sail. They were making progress.

A male voice sounded from the back where he was steering the boat. He said, "My God, that was a shitty night. I got sick, sorry everyone. I hope this trip gets better." The group agreed. He wasn't the only one who had been seasick.

Another man spoke. Like the rest, he was squinting. "Good morning, everyone. It is easier to see your faces in the morning sun. My name is Benito."

From her seat next to him, a round-faced woman with short brown hair said, "It was chaotic when we boarded last night. I didn't realize we would be so rushed to get off the beach." She paused and added, "Oh, I am Benito's wife, Blanca."

"Yeah, that was nuts," said the first woman. She identified herself as Pilar then she said, "When I showed up at Brisas del Mar Beach last night, I expected the boat to be bigger. What is this, seven feet by twelve feet? And look how low the sides are. If it weren't for those rickety posts sticking up around the edge of the boat and the ropes running between them, all of us would have been in the water."

Yadier, an athletic young man wearing a red knock off Adidas jacket added, "Those are called 'lifelines.' I know a little about boats from reading," he said. "You can see where our unknown builders increased buoyancy outside the 'chug,' our homemade boat. Look at those pieces of styrofoam on each side. That big inner tube out front helps as well."

"Why do we have an opening in the boat?" asked Blanca. "I like sitting there and dangling my feet inside the boat, but it takes up space we could use to lie down."

"That half-yard-wide slot running across the boat enables us to look under the deck and see the condition of the structure or 'hull' of the boat," said Yadier. "Remember, this is our only home, and the water can be our enemy. We will need to check in there often to be sure our house is safe."

Benito said, "We can store some things down there on the bottom, yes? This deck is very crowded with people and supplies."

"Maybe, but there isn't much room," said Yadier. "I looked below the deck last night; the boat has a very deep hull but it is packed with large styrofoam pieces and a lot of big empty water bottles with caps. All that is bulky and it is tied down. It will also help with buoyancy if the hull is damaged."

"In addition," he continued, "it is common for chugs to leak water. That water collects in the 'bilge,' the lowest part inside the hull. Maybe we could put food and drinks sealed in glass or plastic down there but nothing else."

Blanca commented about another part of the homemade boat, "Look at the mast. Is that what you call it, Yadier?" He nodded. Blanca continued, "It is made from a tree branch. I hope it is really strong or the wind will shove it down our throats."

Yadier said, "I wondered about that too, so I checked. It appears to be secured to the wooden hull pretty well. I am not as confident about that dirty cotton sail. The lines attached to it seem okay, but the cloth is very old. We will need these oars if the sail is destroyed. I think the biggest problem is the <u>number</u> of us who were packed on this boat."

"Exactly," said Benito. His black hair was very curly after the night's shower. "I was told the boat would have maybe four or five people. We are seven."

"Same for me. This is more crowded than I expected," said Blanca. "We are going to get to know each other very well."

Up front, the tall, quiet muscular man wearing a white t-shirt and headscarf stood up. Then he turned and urinated off the bow. Piss breaks had happened many times during the night, but in the daylight it seemed more offensive.

Pilar said, "Can't you at least do that downwind off the back of the boat?"

Benito said, "Hey you. She's right. Next time do it back here."

He responded. "My name is not 'hey you.' I am Bernardo."

Yadier had been steering for many hours. He asked, "Would someone else do this for a while? I am really tired."

"Sure," said Benito. He stepped carefully over three other passengers as he moved across the boat. Once at the back of the boat he gripped the tiller. Yadier slid away cautiously on the crowded deck.

Small talk continued while most tried to stretch their muscles. Two members of the group had not yet spoken: Santiago, a thin, ashen man in his seventies, and Diego, a fit, distinguished looking man. His poise and calmness seemed to indicate he was well-educated. His thick hair was prematurely gray.

As the day and the boat progressed the sea was calm. It was sunny and warm. The light on the shimmering water was hypnotizing. Many of the group donned wide-brimmed hats as they finished drying off.

"You are smart to wear hats and protect yourselves from the sun. We will be overexposed to sun, rain, wind and the rolling of the seas," said the man with the thick gray hair. My name is Diego. I am a doctor and obviously a refugee like you."

"*Hola* Diego. I think we are lucky to have a doctor with us," said Pilar. The others agreed and greeted Diego.

"Thank you. Later today we can discuss how this voyage will affect us as the days become more difficult," he said, "but for now I ask everyone with vomit on their clothing to rinse it in the sea after wiping up any on the boat. That smell can make us all queasy. One more thing: most people adapt to the motion of the sea. If you were sick last night or if you feel sick now, I believe you will better cope soon. One trick is to look at the horizon instead of the turbulent water close to us."

After the boat was cleaned up, Diego suggested they all bring out the food, supplies and tools they each had brought along. He hoped to compile an inventory for the group's general use. They complied, bumping into one another, then Diego performed the survey.

"Thank you, everyone, for your contributions." Diego came across as an educated, refined man. "We have around thirty gallons of water in the big jug plus some individual bottles, six packs of powdered milk, ten cans of sweet condensed milk, multiple big sacks of nuts and a few cartons of crackers. Here are a couple dry salamis, chunks of cheese, and four round loaves of bread. Here are three big cans of orange juice."

"Who brought the *Juevos con Chorizo?*" asked Yadier to no one in particular. He was being ironic. Everyone feared they would experience food and water shortages. Nobody laughed.

"Shit," said Bernardo, "I could eat all that in a day." He had brought none of the supplies.

"But you won't," snapped Diego as he looked Bernardo in the eyes. "We must regulate our food and water intake. We cannot run out halfway to Florida. We have <u>at least</u> another three days to go." Diego now looked at the group. "Do you all agree?" Nearly all said yes. Bernardo said nothing.

Diego had emerged as the leader. He was also the food sentry. He kept the supplies in a plastic bag near his preferred spot on deck. He put the cans of condensed milk below the deck.

Diego continued. "We also have three boxes of *cigarillos negros*. I assume the smokers brought their own matches or lighters, yes?" Four of the group nodded.

"Now our gear," Diego said. "Obviously, our sail is working. We have four oars for when the wind is not our friend. I am glad everyone hung up the blankets and tarps to dry. We also have soap and three tubes of sunscreen. Very smart, whoever brought that. There are two fishing knives, some fishing gear, pencils and paper. We also have two flashlights with batteries. Let's try to limit the use of them. I brought a GPS, a compass, and a mobile phone. Anyone else bring a phone? We will need them when we arrive in Florida."

"Yes, I have one," said Yadier. Benito nodded. Yadier continued. "I also brought a computer battery and some charger wires. I figured we could recharge the phones if necessary."

Timid, frail Santiago had said nothing, but then he pushed and crawled his way to the back. He unzipped and pee'd off the boat. Soon the other men did the same. The women looked at each other nervously.

Diego summarized their supply situation. "With only a day's notice and no communication among us, we brought along a <u>lot</u> of the right things. I think we should now work out schedules for steering and general watch," he stated. "Even at night—especially at night— we need a helmsman and another person alert for anything unusual. If we lose wind, we will need four people to row."

The midday sun was baking the crew; the temperature approached 95 degrees. They were thankful when the wind picked up.

Diego continued, "Okay if I work out a boat duty schedule?" Nods all around.

"May I assume that you two, Blanca and Benito, would like to be on duty together?" They smiled and nodded.

"Okay, I will work on it," Diego said. "How about toilet protocols? Any ideas?"

Pilar spoke up. "I am assuming nobody wants to go in the water to 'go' though that would work."

Diego said, "We could leave that as an option, right? Anyone going for a swim, however, needs to hold onto a line attached to the boat."

Pilar spoke again. "From the boat, for 'ones' the men have an advantage. How about they just go to the back and wizz downwind? I expect only men will take time on the tiller anyway. For 'twos' they can do the same thing by hanging their butts off the back of the boat. Oh my God, did anyone bring toilet paper?"

"I did," said Blanca. "Five rolls."

Blanca's husband added, "We need to put it somewhere accessible by everyone, but it needs to be kept out of the rain."

"Done," said Blanca. "I'll keep the TP in a plastic shopping bag, but I will leave one roll out when the weather is dry."

Pilar returned to the issue of ladies' potty. It had become personal and urgent. "For the women, actually everybody, how about if that corner of the boat becomes 'potty corner'?" She pointed toward the back of the boat, left side. When one of us women is there doing her business someone else, anyone, has to hold up a blanket for her. Alright?"

Diego looked around. Then he asked, "Is that good with everyone?" Nobody commented, so it became the rule.

"Well then," said Pilar, "I am getting a blanket right now. Who wants to hold it up for me?" Blanca volunteered. When Pilar was done, they switched places.

CHAPTER ELEVEN

Benito changed the subject. "When I was notified about our departure, I was happy the boat was only thirty-five miles from Havana at Brisas del Mar. I was worried I would have to go out west toward Bahia Honda."

Pilar said, "Me too, and I am glad those guys on the beach helped us get the boat in the water. Do you suppose they did that on their own? Or maybe they built the boat and got it to the beach for Carlos, the guy I paid in Havana?"

"We were also contacted by Carlos. He is like a one-way, disposable-boat charterer," said Benito. "Our families in Miami paid a guy there directly. They paid $12,000 for each of us. We couldn't afford that ourselves but we hope to pay them back."

Everyone on board sacrificed much to make the trip, and during preparations they hid their activities from friends and family members. There were snitches everywhere in Cuba. Diego kept quiet about the money. He paid a premium rate of $18,000 due to the Cuban government's ongoing, energetic search for him. There was a price on his head.

Pilar asked, "Did anyone consider flying to Bogotá then making your way to Mexico to cross into the U.S.? Most are doing that now."

"No way," said Benito. "Because of pressure by the Americans, the Mexicans are stopping most foreigners at the California and Texas borders. Some friends tried an overland land trip. Then got put in an awful detention center, and they were stuck there for six months while their circumstances were being considered. After all their trouble, they got sent back."

Santiago commented softly, "I am a boater—a *balsero*. It is the safest way now."

Though it appeared everyone was boating for the same reasons, Benito continued. The rest were courteous listeners at least for now.

"Under the wet-foot, dry-foot policy, if you made it to land, you stayed. If you got stopped on the water, you got sent home. It was simple. Even with that policy gone I prefer my chances in Florida waters or on Florida land. I heard that once you make it to Florida, the Americans often assume you are a political refugee. While they evaluate your case, you stay at the Migration and Refugee Services in Miami. I think it is run by a religious group. I've heard they at least provide food and a place to sleep."

"Speaking of food," said Pilar, "I am getting hungry and thirsty."

She was not alone. The crew suggested that Diego distribute the food and water and that they all eat at the same time. Except for a few plastic bottles, the water was stored in a big gray insulated jug hanging off the back of the boat. Diego served small portions with plastic cups someone brought aboard. He gave more to those who had vomited; they needed rehydration.

He retrieved the bread and said, "Let's agree that we eat only twice a day, at least early in our journey. Today we started eating late. I will present the first meal earlier tomorrow."

He continued. "We will have water three times per day, and I will distribute it. We don't want to run out nor do we want the food to be taken by just one person or by just a few of us. We must remain smart about these things." He took silence to mean agreement. Diego portioned out the bread and cheese, the most perishable of their foodstuff. Most of the crew were satisfied. Bernardo was not.

"Jesus, man. I can't live on that," he barked, "I am twice the size of them. How is that fair?"

Diego said, "Bernardo, I understand you are a big man. Here, take just a little bit more bread, but that is all. We cannot have this argument at every meal." Bernardo winced, then took the added scrap of bread.

Diego became philosophical. He said, "I am sure we have differing views about religion, but right now with this bread and water let's take a moment to be silent or pray if you like. Let's think about the journey ahead of us. We will need luck and Divine guidance to make it to Florida safely."

A few moments passed. The chatter resumed as the immigrants settled in further like a box of cats. They shared personal stories and reasons for making the perilous trip. Blanca was the first to speak bluntly about leaving Cuba.

"Cubans are industrious people, but our country is so badly managed there are no opportunities for personal initiative to make life better. I want more in life. The government puts limits on all of us. They don't encourage innovation and progress; they crush it. We are prisoners. Here we are in fear, risking everything to escape that prison. Our <u>leaders</u> should be the prisoners for what they are doing to the Cuban people."

"Absolutely," said Pilar. "Havana was once a world class city, but it has been decaying since the revolution. Yes, we were happy to flush out corruption, but in the end we learned that communism does not work. Our buildings are falling down and water and power services are unreliable."

"I agree. Communism was just a different form of corruption. Our political and military leaders live a much nicer life than the rest of us," said Benito. "We must wait in lines to get basic foods. Often the shops are bare, and the products we buy are substandard and poorly made."

Javier spoke up. "All that is true, and I am glad we are on our way to a better life. But I will miss my family. That is a very high price to pay for basic freedoms." Others in the group nodded their agreement.

The talk of home wound down. According to the newly established schedule, big Bernardo relieved Benito at the tiller. Diego's wristwatch was fastened to a spar. Others who were scheduled for active roles in the night were informed. Concerned about old Santiago's health, Diego slid nearer him. Santiago seemed unfit for the journey.

"Hello my friend. How are you feeling?" Before Santiago could answer, Diego felt his forehead and checked his pulse.

"I am feeling tired. I did not sleep last night. I was very cold and wet. The sunshine today feels very nice, and it helped to eat and drink water."

Diego said, "If you feel worse, please tell me. I will be happy to help you. May I ask, why did you sign up for such a difficult trip?"

"My children and grandchildren are all in Florida. I want to be with them in my final years. They are all I care about. Can you understand?"

"Of course," said Diego, "family is very important. I am sure they will be happy to see you. Please stay warm tonight. I will make sure you have your own blanket." After that, Diego moved away. He was very concerned about Santiago's health.

Before the evening meal and before darkness fell, Diego and Yadier checked the condition of the boat. It was still in good shape; no loose boards or fittings. The lifelines—ropes running through holes in boards protruding twenty inches above the deck—were still taut.

The added pieces of foam were still tightly tied to the boat. The inner tube was firm. Their big water jug was hanging in the water, and it was tied securely to the back of the boat. Its lid was tightly sealed. Everything below the deck was solid and in place, and the boat's crude bilge was surprisingly dry. The boat was holding up well so far.

The crew received food, cheese and water. Again Bernardo complained, but his ration was kept equal to the others.

"Hey Diego," said Blanca, "you said you would tell us more about what to expect on this trip."

Diego said, "Yes, thank you. Most of you probably know this crossing will be difficult for our bodies and our minds. We already experienced seasickness and nausea. Hopefully, as I suggested before, that will subside. We talked briefly about sun protection; we Cubans know a lot about that, but on the sea, the reflection off the water will magnify the sun's effects on us. We have sunscreen, so use it.

"There will be other effects from constant exposure to the wind, rain and sea: dehydration, eye pain and maybe vision problems and headaches. Fatigue will become our worst enemy. It will create stress, reduce our immunity and cloud our decisions. Some of us will become angry, others may have hallucinations." Diego stopped. The crew looked worried.

After a pause, Yadier asked, "Are there ways we can deal with these problems? You make them sound unavoidable."

"I was just about to mention some ideas. Thank you for your question," replied Diego. He sounded professorial. "When the sea allows, stand and stretch muscles; even do that when sitting. If it doesn't make you sick, close and cover your eyes regularly. Rub each others' shoulders and neck. When it is cold, sit nearer each other. Embrace each other to retain heat. Let's work as a group for emotional support. Talk to each other; there are no secrets on our tiny island. Share your concerns and support each other."

Before nightfall, Diego powered up his GPS to check their position. Considering the previous night's slow start, rain and turbulent winds, they had progressed well. He informed everyone they had travelled twenty-nine miles from Brisas del Mar.

The group cheered. Benito said, "Key West is, what 105 miles from Havana? We'll be there on Friday."

"*Bueno,*" said Pilar.

"Wait wait," said Diego, "yes, we went a long distance in roughly one day, but the strong current in the Florida Straits pushed us east. After I reversed the GPS setting to show our remaining distance to Key West, I see we still have 100 miles to go." Everyone was confused and they talked over each other.

Pilar spoke above the din. "At this rate it will take us another twenty days or so. We will be dead by then." Again the group erupted into crosstalk.

Diego raised his hand and his voice, "My friends, please, let's discuss this." The group got quieter while he checked something on the GPS.

He looked up from the GPS screen and said, "Maybe the current can be our friend."

Benito reacted immediately. "How can it be our friend? That makes no sense." The others voiced agreement.

"If we keep trying to sail east," Diego said, each day will be a struggle. Remember last night, it was rainy, but we had lots of wind in our sail. Imagine a day with very little wind; we will make zero progress, maybe even drift further from Key West."

"So what do we do?" Asked Blanca. She looked exasperated.

Diego said, "We should sail north. With the current, the boat will go to the northeast, toward the middle of the Florida Keys, maybe the Upper Keys. It is further, but the current will get us there faster."

"How much further?"

"At least fifty miles to the Middle Keys, more if we land in Key Largo."

Javier, "This <u>still</u> makes no sense. We need to go to Key West, because it is closer. We just need to compensate with our heading."

"Javier, if we do that, we will never reach land," said Benito. "Diego is right, it is not <u>how far</u> we go, it is <u>how far in the right direction</u> we go. Do the math. Because of the current, we sailed only five percent of the way to Key West in the past day, but we sailed roughly twenty percent of the way to the Middle Keys."

The others were processing Javier's comments. Diego said, "Correct, my friend. We can make landfall in three more days. We have the supplies for that."

"I hoped it wouldn't take that long," said Blanca.

Pilar reassured her. "Together we can do this," she said. Diego could read that Blanca was scared, and he knew the trip was going to become more difficult and stressful.

Diego spoke again. "There is another benefit to landing in the Middle Keys: fewer Coast Guard and Navy boats on the water. Because of its relative size and its location, Key West has a <u>lot</u> of military activity, but there isn't much between Key West and Key Largo, the two big towns."

Diego continued, "So, is everyone okay with changing our objective?" The others agreed. "We will have to change our course from time to time. We don't want to drift too far east and end up in the Atlantic."

Everyone seemed to follow the logic. Diego's arguments were informed and compelling. Despite the prospect of longer distances, they relaxed and settled for the night. The moon on the water created a spectacular, luminous effect. The air was humid and salty; birds flew by hoping for scraps of food. Their second night was expected to be a smooth, dry one.

John Gordon

CHAPTER TWELVE

Art was already on the balcony enjoying the sunny, calm morning. Jackson opened the slider and stepped outside to join him. He sat to discuss the day's plans. "Another perfect morning in paradise," he said.

"Yup. Looks like a boating day unless you wanna be a tourist," replied Art.

"Boating. We can't pass that up on a day like this."

"Sounds good to me. Let's go on the ocean side today. You are gonna like that a lot," said Art.

"Okay, I'll scrounge some breakfast and be ready in forty-five minutes. We really should get more groceries today."

"Take your time, Jackie. No rush."

After the guys had breakfast, they showered, dressed and prepared the boat bag. Art turned on the power to the boat lift. After prepping the boat, Art and Jackson were again underway and heading north. Their plan was to enter nearby Blackwater Sound, cross it to the east and take the Adams Cut to the ocean side. After only a few minutes underway and just entering Blackwater Sound, the engine stalled.

"That's weird," said Art.

"Maybe the cooling water intake is clogged and the engine overheated and shut down," said Jackson.

"Could be, I guess, although we would have heard an alarm just before the engine quit." Art put the throttle in neutral, and he tried to restart the engine. No luck. He raised the outboard motor and looked at the intake ports. Everything seemed okay.

Meanwhile the wind stiffened; the boat was lying adrift and floating downwind toward Boggy Key. Art knew they didn't have much time before the boat ran aground. He quickly checked the depth sounder reading, then he moved to the bow and opened the anchor locker. He pulled out the heavy Danforth anchor. It was attached to the boat by fifteen feet of chain then seventy-five feet of line. Art lowered the anchor into the water hand over hand until he paid out forty-five feet of chain and line. It was the right length given the water depth and the conditions of the sea. Then he wrapped the anchor line around the cleat at the bow and waited. The boat's bow slowly turned toward the anchor and the boat stopped drifting backwards. Those were indications that the anchor had set and was holding well to the grassy seabed. Now that the boat was secure, Art and Jackson tried to resolve the engine issue.

"What the heck," said Jackson, "clogged fuel filter? The way the engine loped before stopping, it seemed like it was starving."

"Yeah. I heard that too, but I just had a full service done four months ago. Since then, it has been run only a few hours.

Vulnerable parts like a fuel filter get cleaned or replaced, and we haven't been aground or sucked up sand."

Jackson said, "Let's take off the engine cowling. Maybe a wire or hose came loose."

"Okay," said Art. He and Jackson flipped the cowling latches and removed the heavy gray fiberglass cover. They set it on the forward deck. Both men scanned the engine.

"It looks pristine, like new," said Jackson. "I don't see any disconnections or leaky fluids. Wadda you think, Art?"

"I agree. That is showroom condition. I am glad but now more perplexed. Let's put the cowling back on so we don't trip over it."

After replacing the cowling, Jackson offered another possibility. "Bad or contaminated fuel?"

"Possible, I guess, but not likely. I try to keep the tank full to limit internal condensation," said Art. "We are sorta down on fuel, but I don't think that's a problem. Besides, the new fuel filter would help with that."

Jackson said, "I don't smell fuel. I don't think there is a leak. We can check the bilge to be sure, though I don't know why a leak would stop the engine. More likely, the boat would just explode." Art winced, then he opened a hatch for a look and sniff. No fuel leak.

Art sat and looked at his feet. Both were silent for a few minutes. Finally, Art said, "Let's take one last look around the boat. If we don't solve the problem, I'll call BoatUS for a tow. I'm glad I bought the 'unlimited' package. Towing is fuggin' expensive."

Separately they moved around the boat. Ed looked in the center console; he checked for loose wires behind the switch panel. Jackson looked inside hatches. Running out of ideas, they started knocking on the hull, inside and out.

Jackson bent over the port side to look for oil or gas in the water. There was none, but he discovered something else. "Art, come look at this," he yelled.

Art leaned over the fuel fill cap and looked at the hull where Jackson was pointing. "That is the fuel tank breather port. Damn, it has some gunk in it. What is that?" He leaned over again, this time further to pull off some of the gunk; Jackson held onto the back of his belt for safety. Art stood back up and felt and smelled the material.

"It's sticky and it smells like bubblegum," Art said. "Shit, it _is_ bubble gum." With wide eyes he looked at Jackson.

"Bubble gum? On the venting port?" said Jackson. "That would explain the engine quitting."

"That's true. But how did it get there? I've never heard of gum in the water magically attaching itself like a barnacle."

"And it was way above the waterline. Someone had to put it there," said Jackson. "Could someone else, maybe a prankster have messed with the boat at the house?"

Art responded quickly. "It's possible. The boat was high on the rack and the lift was turned off. Someone could have reached up to that port if they were tall enough. Or they could have used a step stool."

"But who would want to do that? Was it a random prank, or did you piss off someone?"

Art paused a beat, then he looked at Jackson and said, "No, but you did."

Jackson remembered the confrontation on Sunday night at the Lions Club. His ever-queasy stomach silently wailed, but he challenged the theory.

"If you are thinking that Racist Ed did this, how would he know you and where you live?"

"Jackie, you introduced me to the crowd, you said my name. You wanted me to be recognized, and I appreciated that. He heard my name or got it again after the dust-up at Mrs. Mac's. You've seen that people around here know me. I'm not easy to ignore. And remember, I smacked him around harder than you did at Mrs. Mac's."

"So, somehow he found you?" asked Jackson. Art was nodding while Jackson spoke. "And he came over last night while we were asleep." More nodding. "So how did we get this far before the engine quit?"

"Just enough air in the system to keep the fuel flowing for a bit, I guess," said Art.

"I didn't hear anyone on the dock last night, did you?" asked Jackson.

"We wouldn't," said Art. "We sleep at the other end of the house, the A/C is always on, and my double-pane hurricane windows could fully muffle an explosion." Jackson shook his head. *This is weird.*

Art picked out the rest of the gum, rolled it into a ball and placed it into a stainless steel cup holder. The men went to the helm. Art eased the engine's lower unit into the water. He confirmed the throttle was still in neutral, then he turned the key. The engine jumped to life, and it ran smoothly.

Art was giddy. He did a parody of Dr. Frankenstein and shouted, "It's alive, it's alive!"

Jackson laughed out loud although he was a mess. Between his chronic gut pain, the breakdown, the boat's uncomfortable motion, and now the stalker, he wanted to swim in a pool of Pepto Bismol. "Can we go home now, daddy?" he asked.

Art said, "I gotta get some food. It is way past lunchtime. Jimmy Johnson's is a good place and it is just over there." Art was pointing across Blackwater Sound.

CHAPTER THIRTEEN

In a few minutes they were performing a tricky maneuver at the restaurant's short dock. The shallow water made it even more challenging. Art raised the outdrive slightly to protect his propeller, and Jackson readied the lines and fenders. They worked out the docking process; they always talked about docking before they took action.

"Jackie, we've done this before. I'm going in perpendicular to the dock. Then I'm gonna nudge up to that piling." He pointed to the targeted post.

"I'll be at the bow to fend," said Jackson. "Then I'll get a line around the piling and make it off on the bow cleat."

"Right. In neutral, I will direct the prop toward the dock. Signal me when the bow line is secured, and steady yourself. I will give the engine a bump of reverse, and the stern will float right in. I'll handle the stern line. You stay at the bow," Art said.

The docking went as planned. They collected their wallets and the boat key then they stepped off the boat onto the boardwalk leading to the restaurant's outside deck. Art was a regular at Jimmy Johnson's as well. He waved to his favorite server, Marie. She was carrying a large food tray, so she simply smiled and nodded. They seated themselves. The full name of the place was Jimmy Johnson's Big Chill.

Jackson asked, "Is he the same Jimmy Johnson who coached the Miami Dolphins?"

"That's him. He's a big-time fisherman, and he is a sports legend in South Florida. He coached the University of Miami to a national championship before coaching the Dolphins."

"Also some Super Bowl wins, right?" asked Jackson.

"Two in a row with the Dallas Cowboys. He's a Hall of Famer and now an analyst for Sunday pro games. After lunch we'll go inside the bar. There is memorabilia everywhere."

"I'd like that," said Jackson. "I assume the food is good or we wouldn't be here, right?"

"The food is very good. So is the service. Marie's been here a long time. She is a sweetheart, funny and smart."

 Marie approached and said, "Hi Art. How are you? It's been a while."

"Hi Marie, it's great to see you. Yeah, I was stuck in California. Marie, this is my best buddy, Jackson. He's a boat guy like me."

"Hi Jackson. Welcome to Key Largo. I hope you like it here."

"I love it here, though it helps to have a friend who knows the best places."

Marie put her hand lightly on Art's shoulder and said, "We love having Art stop by when he is in town. We also love it when he brings us new customers." She laughed, then she asked, "May I start you with drinks?"

"I think two Bud Lights for us," said Jackson. He glanced at Art for agreement and he got it.

When the beers arrived, Art raised his bottle. "Jackie, here's to not having to call BoatUS." They touched bottles and Jackson managed a smile. "Ahhh, nice water, good eats, and friendly people," said Art. Art ordered a pulled pork sandwich; Jackson decided on grilled snapper.

They could see from the deck that the boat was fine. The lines and fenders remained secure. After eating their sandwiches, Art had a piece of Key Lime Pie. Jackson passed on the pie. The rich dessert sounded great, but he avoided taxing his stomach. After the pie Jackson paid. Marie hugged them both as they headed to the boat. Jackson and Art reversed the docking process, and they pulled away. The boat's name garnered a few cheers from diners on Big Chill's restaurant deck.

Art smacked the steering wheel and grunted. Then he said, "Jackie, I am so sorry. I forgot to show you Jimmy's 'egotorium' in the bar. Dammit."

"No worries. We'll just have to come back," said Jackson.

Art shoved the throttle hard forward, and they headed for home. In twenty minutes they were back at the dock. Art buttoned up the boat and he raised it unusually high with the lift. In the house, he turned off the boat lift circuit breaker. He tossed the wad of gum in the trash. Then they both cooled off and relaxed on the balcony.

Jackson was bothered by the boat tampering. He said, "That business with the gum, does that kind of thing happen much around here?" He was hoping for an explanation other than nasty Ed.

"Engines get stolen. That's why I like my boat high on the lift," he said. "Mischief? Maybe, it happens, but I haven't heard a lot about it. Like I said, it could've been kids." Art was also concerned, but he didn't want Jackson freaking out more.

"I can understand kids tossing mud or spraying graffiti, but plugging the venting port? They'd have to know about boat systems to know that would cause a problem on the water. I'm thinking it was more than a random prank," said Jackson.

"Kids around here grow up on boats, but I get it, Jackie. Kids or not, it pisses me off. We'll just have to keep an eye on things from now on. Maybe we also run the boat for a while at the dock next time before pushing off, just to see if she is okay."

Jackson changed the subject. "Art, do you have something like Tums?"

He stood and said, "Yeah, I think so. Follow me."

Art pulled down a plastic container of Tums from a cupboard above the split sink. "Here you go Jackie, take 'em all if you need to."

Jackson took a few and placed the bottle in a conspicuous place on the marble counter. "Okay if I leave them here? I suspect I'll come back for more."

"No worries, Jackie. I hope you feel better."

Jackson said, "Thanks, me too. I'm gonna go lie down for a bit."

"Sure," said Art, "I may do that myself." He did. They both slept the rest of the afternoon. Around 6:00 PM, Art heard Jackson stirring in the living room, so he joined him.

Art said, "Well that felt good. How ya feeling, Jackie?"

"Better, thanks, good enough to get a couple hours' sleep." A moment passed. "Pwah," he uttered, "what now, dinner?"

"Sure, it'll have to be takeout again," said Art. "I'm not up for mingling. I'm questioning the honor of humanity right now." He was referring to the boat vandal. He knew it was also on Jackson's mind.

Jackson chuckled. "There are tiny-minded people everywhere, it seems. Takeout is okay with me. Do they make Tums Pizza here? Kidding. I can eat something that's not too greasy."

"You may have noticed that fried foods are a thing here. Maybe we can get you a baguette to gnaw on," said Art. "I know we have been to Hobo's, but their food is great, and I have a copy of their take-out menu." He opened a drawer in the kitchen. It contained a stack of colorful, folded menus. After rifling through them, Art pulled out the one for Hobo's.

"Maybe we can get them to make us Monte Cristo sandwiches," he said. "It's ham, turkey, and swiss cheese between two slices of French toast, sprinkled with powdered sugar. I didn't think of it when we were there. It is rarely on the menu, but the chef is kind enough to make one for me when he has the ingredients. Good guy. Sometimes they don't have powdered sugar for the finish, so I keep some here. How does that sound, Jackson?"

"Ooh, I'll have one for sure as long as they don't deep fry the whole thing. That is gross."

"Nuh nuh nuh," replied Art. "These are light and tasty. You'll love it. Fries, salad?"

"Nope."

Art placed the order; he added a Ceasar salad for himself. Jackson agreed to do the pickup. In thirty-five minutes the food was on the table.

"This is great, really great," said Jackson. His stomach was cooperating, not complaining.

"Agreed. Hobo's is good every time. Fortunately, we have lots more good places here. We may <u>never</u> have to get groceries at Publix, although my breakfasts are getting more creative. I'm not sure I have anything suitable for breakfast in the freezer; frozen fettuccine isn't really a breakfast food is it?" Jackson shook his head. His mouth was full.

After dinner, they plopped onto the white couches again. Art switched on the television and asked, "How about a movie tonight?

I recorded *Breaking Away*, that biking film about those kids—those 'cutters'—in Indiana."

"Don't think I've seen it, sure."

"Jackie!" Art said. "I know you haven't lived in a tool shed since the mid-seventies. How can you not know about *Breaking Away*? Paul Dooley is fantastic in it, and Dennis Quaid is only, like eighteen."

Jackson could also play the cinephile. "Well Art, after seeing the groundbreaking, seven-hour, Russian color production of Tolstoi's 1967 film, *War and Peace*, I figured everything else would smell of fertilizer."

"Alright, alright. I'll quit being a dick. But we're gonna watch *Breaking Away* and <u>you</u> are gonna love it." Art retrieved the film in his saved file and they watched it nonstop. Jackson laughed a lot. Art was vindicated.

Despite the naps, the guys retired after the movie. Jackson took his time removing his watch and brushing his teeth. *I sure hope we don't have any more of that sabotage. I didn't come here to be hassled.*

Art returned to the living room, opened the slider and gazed at Miami's distant, faint glow reflected on the water outside. *When we find the bastard who messed with my boat, I may need to smack him around.*

CHAPTER FOURTEEN

As they had hoped, the Cuban refugees enjoyed a calm, dry night aboard the makeshift lumber boat. They were still adjusting to the crowded conditions and the constant movement, so they slept fitfully. The duty shifts kept them on course. The subtropical sun warmed the waking passengers.

They were greeted by Diego's voice. The self-appointed navigator had checked their progress on his GPS. He broke the silence. "Good morning everybody. Even with light winds overnight we are now fifty-four miles from Cuba and on a good course."

His shipmates were satisfied, at least as satisfied as they could be after a night exposed on a splintered wooden deck. The group offered a low-volume cheer.

Diego continued, "As expected, the current is pushing us to the east. We may make a slight course change."

Benito asked, "That is no problem, right?"

"No problem," said Diego, "but we can only estimate the new course. Then we will adjust again if necessary."

The group went about their morning rituals on the cramped boat: stretching, rubbing sore muscles, folding blankets, washing with seawater, toilet duties off the back of the boat. When the chores were finished and the passengers were settled, Diego said, "I am sure everyone is hungry and thirsty. We will take some water now, and we will have our first meal in one hour." There were a few groans; ever-hungry Bernardo said, "Shit man, another hour? We're hungry <u>now</u>, dude."

"We do have some crude fishing gear, and we could use salami as bait," said Diego. "Someone should give it a try today. More food means bigger meals."

"I will do it today. I like to fish and I like to eat fish," said Bernardo. The group spoke their thanks.

Curly-haired Benito said, "Shouldn't we make that course change soon?"

"Yes," Yadier answered for Diego. "It is my turn at the tiller, so I will make a correction of fifteen degrees to the west from our current heading. We can check it again before nightfall." Diego thanked him.

After everyone finished their morning rations of water, bread and cheese, outspoken Pilar said what was on the minds of most onboard. "Diego, you have become our leader because of the way you speak and behave. You are smart, educated, and *muy simpatico.*"

"*Gracias,*" he said.

Pilar continued, "You haven't told us why you are on the boat. Working doctors like you have a good life in Cuba. Many other people become educated as doctors, but they drive taxis and do other jobs. So why are you leaving Cuba and your family?"

He suspected such questions would surface during the trip, but Diego didn't want to discuss his motives. He said, "As with all of you, I am sure, it is complicated."

This time big Bernardo spoke. Not surprising, he was blunt. "Yeah, you sound like a big shot. We would love to have your life. But here you are with us. Why?"

"I am not a big shot at all. We all know that Cuba has more doctors than it needs. We send doctors to other countries for energy and other supplies." *This is getting uncomfortable. I should have kept my mouth shut.*

Although the others weren't as outspoken as Bernardo, they hadn't heard a reason for Diego to make the dangerous and expensive trip to Florida. <u>Everyone</u> had a reason. Diego stayed silent while he pondered what to say. *We are in the middle of the ocean without a way to communicate to others. These people, by their being here, dislike the corrupt Cuban government. I guess I have nothing to lose by telling them the truth. Ultimately, I may need their help.*

"It is a long story, but I will tell you. We don't have much else to do anyway but remain alive for the next few days," said Diego. "As with my fellow doctors, some of my patients are high-level government officials. Some of them work for the 'DI,' the Cuban intelligence service. I have other patients who work for the Ministry of the Revolution Armed Forces of Cuba."

"So you are a spy?" asked Bernardo.

CHAPTER FIFTEEN

Despite the rising tension, Diego remained calm. He shushed them then he said, "I am not a spy. We are on the same side. Please let me finish." He paused.

"As I said, I am just a doctor, a general practitioner. At my office, I work to maintain the health of my patients, and I focus on education. But, sometimes when the bosses were very busy, I went to <u>their</u> offices to give them physical exams and conduct follow-up visits. I also helped them get their medications. While I was there I sometimes overheard them talking. I was there so often, I was like furniture. They stopped searching me whenever I entered the facility.

"Most of the time they made boring conversation about budgets or logistics. Often they just complained about their work. They even told me how frustrated they were. They saw me as another professional behind the big walls, and they told me secrets.

"I should say that it was not just me getting a peek inside these departments. My fellow doctors—the anti-government ones who also spend time at DI and MINFAR—shared information with me. Over the past year and based on all we heard and saw, the other doctors and I worked at putting together the pieces. Our conclusions were disturbing."

Diego's audience was rapt. "So what did you find out?" asked Blanca.

Diego's response was as troubling as it was blunt. "Our government is in the process of securing a chemical weapon called Sarin," he said.

Some of the immigrants expressed shock. Benito said, "What? Why would they do that? That makes no sense."

"Isn't that some kind of killer gas?" asked Bernardo.

"Sarin is a man-made chemical, a liquid. When released, it evaporates quickly and spreads as a gas. Its victims ingest it and have immediate, often fatal reactions. Over twenty-five years ago, it was also used in a subway terrorist attack in Japan. After that it was banned pretty much worldwide. However, the Syrians were accused of using it a couple times within this decade."

"I thought those nerve gas supplies were destroyed," said Blanca.

"Yes. Along with more than 160 other countries, Cuba signed the Convention on the Prohibition of the Development, Production, Stockpiling and Use of Chemical Weapons and on their Destruction, which went into force in 1997. The Cuban legislature reaffirmed its commitment to that agreement in 2011. Today, 193 countries claim to abide by this agreement."

Benito returned to his previous question. "So why would people in government want this poison?"

"They might use it against a perceived outside threat to our country or against the Cuban people," Diego said.

"Against Cubans?" said Blanca. She was incredulous. "Why the hell would they do that?"

"Some people fear the future, Blanca." Diego cleared his throat, then he continued. "Raul Castro is eighty-nine years old. He has been First Secretary of the Communist Party, our top leader, since Fidel died a couple years ago. That same month, Raul stated that he would retire in 2021 and that his successor as First Secretary would be our current President, Miguel Díaz-Canel."

"Of course we know Diaz-Canel. He is young and charismatic. Why is he a problem?" asked Benito.

Diego said, "He is a reformer. We have already seen this in his role as President and as head of the Council of State and the Council of Ministers. What we like about him worries some other people in power. He says he will still preserve Cuba's communist system, <u>but</u> he also talks about making the government more responsive to the people. He mentions modernizing the social and economic systems. The old guard fears he will move Cuba toward legitimate elections, expand ownership of private property, maybe even move us toward a supply-and-demand economy. If that happens, the military and intelligence agencies will have far less influence."

"The military and intelligence services are worried about Diaz-Canal, so they are making Sarin to use on citizens? I don't understand that," said Bernardo.

"Bernardo, they are not making Sarin, they are buying it from Syria and using our allies in Caracas as intermediaries. The Venezuelans are almost as dirty as the Syrians."

Diego continued, "As for why our military would use it domestically, it could be to eliminate progressives in the government. It could also be used on the public to create chaos and fear. Believing the attacks came from outside our island, Cubans would look to the military and intelligence services for security and protection. The military would then use the chaos as a basis to take over the government. If that happens, progress for the Cuban people will be pushed back decades."

Diego continued by anticipating the next question. "So what does that have to do with my being on this boat? I have proof of these terrible plans. On a thumb drive I have photographs of critical classified documents. The military leaders found out I have this information, so they put a price on my head over two months ago. I have been hiding in the southeast with trusted friends. They arranged this passage, and they got me a small GPS device and a mobile phone to use in the United States. A few of my colleagues feared it was too dangerous for me to make a trip like this. They believe the government knows the details about these boat launches —Carlos is probably informing them—and they watch for and capture political dissidents who try to leave. Obviously, I made it this far."

"So what do you plan to do with this information? Do you have influential friends in the U.S.?" asked Pilar.

"I plan to take it to the American congresswoman representing South Miami. That district is seventy percent Latino, mostly

Cubans. It is urgent that I do this soon. The liberals in the U.S. Congress are holding hearings; they intend to improve relations and expand trade with our country. That initiative began after President Obama visited in 2016, when he declared publicly, <u>but incorrectly</u>, that Cuba was no longer a state sponsor of terrorism. Ironically, Obama's naive statement emboldened those in our government to expand terrorism as a legitimate form of defense."

Benito said, "So, you believe Cuba might use Sarin against a 'perceived outside threat'?"

"Yes, but I think it would need to be an <u>existential</u> threat to Cuba as a nation. The moral stigma of using Sarin lasts a very long time. Cuba would be considered a rogue nation like Syria. We would be isolated diplomatically and economically. So you see," said Diego, "whether our government uses Sarin domestically or internationally, it would be a disaster for the Cuban people."

Diego paused. The others were horrified and speechless. Blanca covered her mouth, Benito and others lowered their heads; Bernardo stared into the water. Santiago buried his face in his hands and sobbed.

"I should stop now," said Diego, "I know this is a lot for you to consider. We can discuss it more at a later time. For now, let's focus on getting to Florida safely. I noticed that the wind has picked up and clouds are gathering."

The boaters discussed the implications of what they just heard. Whether against a foreign enemy or their fellow Cubans, the specter of poison gas was repulsive and barbaric to them. Yadier didn't comment nor react during Diego's shocking disclosures. After Diego finished, however, he smugly dismissed the possibility of Sarin gas in Cuba.

"I don't believe these stories," he said. "These fantasy stories are like a puzzle that was put together incorrectly." Diego said nothing.

Pilar said, "I believe what Diego said, and it makes me glad I am going to the United States. I love my homeland, but I do not think our government does what is best for the Cuban people. To them, it is more about ideology than the rights and needs of the people." Except for Yadier, the others appeared to agree with her.

With the discussion ended, Diego served water. In the late afternoon, the wind blew harder and its direction shifted to the southeast. The sea became rougher. The clouds got darker and lower; a storm was coming. Yadier was still working the tiller, and it became more difficult.

Bernardo turned his focus from fishing and said, "Hey boss. Getting hungry over here. If we are gonna eat, we better do it before it rains." He hadn't caught any fish for the food supply.

"Yes, yes. Let's get to that right now." Diego pulled out the food stash. He distributed the remaining bread, some salami plus some nuts. He also gave water to everyone. Despite the disappointing results that day, Diego saved some salami for fish bait.

Benito took over the tiller. Yadier stood briefly to stretch, but the boat's rocking encouraged him to sit like the rest. Everyone started preparing for rain; they spread the blankets and tarps. They also secured all loose items. Diego confirmed the watch schedule, and each of the smokers had another *cigarillo* before the rain.

Diego powered up the GPS to check their progress. "News, my friends: we have travelled eighty-three miles so far." There was a muted reaction; their mood reflected the darkening sky. Diego slowly moved, then he sat well away from Yadier. His cavalier attitude and denial of the Sarin threat bothered Diego.

After sunset, the wind and rain increased. The boat was tossed violently and water entered the bilge. Of course, there was no pump for removing it. After thirty minutes, the rain subsided. Everyone on board was relieved but somewhat shaken. Their faces were pale and their clothes were soaked. Though a couple of them brought other clothing items, it was senseless to change. Water was still sloshing around the deck.

"That was a squall," said Benito. "There will be more, so prepare for them."

Benito was correct. Throughout the night, squalls slammed the chug. Sometimes they were so violent, most of the crew screamed. The ratty boat creaked with each large wave; it became a haunting sound, as if foretelling disaster. Between each storm, the crew checked and again secured their possessions. After a particularly nasty squall, Yadier examined the boat to the extent he could.

He said, "The mast is holding firm, but there is a lot of seawater in the bilge. Our cans of condensed milk are okay, but they are rolling around."

Blanca asked, "The water down below, it can sink us, right?"

Benito responded to his wife. "*Bonita mia*, water below is not good, but we also have items down there that float, the sealed empty bottles and the styrofoam. We also have floating things attached to the outside of the boat. Those things help us a lot. Please do not worry."

"Between the storms," Yadier suggested, "we can bail water using our hats and drinking cups. Let's be ready to do that after the next storm."

Diego said, "Yadier is right. Let's all help."

Another storm raged above them. After it passed and as discussed, the crew formed a system to bail the water. Bernardo and Yadier, the men with the longest arms, reached below and scooped water with hats and cups. They passed the full containers to Diego and Benito to dump overboard. While the water was being dumped, Blanca and Pilar returned empty hats to Bernardo and Yadier to scoop more water.

Despite the storms, threats and discomforts, the crew maintained an upbeat mood. The boat was holding together. It stayed afloat, but it made little progress. Mercifully, after midnight the storms stopped. Diego was at the tiller. Pilar was on watch. Everyone else slept until sunrise.

CHAPTER SIXTEEN

It was 10 AM when Ed Melnik's cell phone rang. Caller ID told him it was Lenny, so he answered with his all-too-familiar line, "Hey Lenny, how's it hangin?"

Lenny feigned a laugh and said, "Ed, you are the most profane man I know." Ed took it as a compliment.

"I knew it was you, Lenmeister. What's up?"

"Look Ed, I need another excuse to get outta the house. I <u>must</u> get away from Helen. Can we try lunch again? My plans for today fell through."

"I have some stuff to do; Thursdays can be busy for me. But, I'm havin' eye trouble: I can't see doin' that shit today." Ed laughed at his own joke. Lenny even chuckled.

"Great," said Lenny, "Mrs. Mac's again or someplace else?"

"After the noisy run-in with those California jagoffs, I got the stink eye when we were leavin' Mrs. Mac's. I vote for someplace else. Bayside Grill? It'd be nice to have a view of the water. Okay?"

"Yes. Is 11:30 alright? I am famished," Lenny said.

"Sure, see you then."

Ninety minutes later, they met at Bayside Grill's second-deck restaurant on the bay side of Key Largo. There was a beach bar and a small boat dock below the restaurant. The eatery offered a million dollar view to the west, beyond Buttonwood Sound and the Intracoastal Waterway. Ed had brought along binoculars. Ed and Lenny ordered; their food arrived promptly.

"Helen's makin' you a crazy man," said Ed. "Did you ever consider makin' a change?"

"Oh, I couldn't do that to her. Truth is we need each other, although she gets in inexplicably weird moods sometimes."

"That's the 'XX Syndrome,' buddy," said Ed, "a whole genetic thing. All women are sometimes crazy like that. The Mexicans invented Dos Equis, so we'd have a special beer to help us cope."

Lenny changed the subject. "I hope we don't run into those Californians again. I doubt they know an anchor from a boat hook. The big guy with the crew cut acted like a total jerk." *But so did you, Ed. I hope that was the last of it.*

"Well, their boat may not be runnin' so good now. I slipped over to their place and made a simple 'adjustment' to their fuel system."

"You went to their house? You messed with their boat? Stuff like that will get you shot in the Keys," said Lenny. "How did you even find them?" Ed was a good boating companion, but sometimes Lenny wondered why they remained friends.

"The joys of public records, my friend," said Ed. "When that Jackson guy gave his talk at the Lions Club, he introduced his friend, Art Prichard.

Those are the guys we saw at Mrs. Mac's. Jackson said that the big Prichard guy has a house in Key Largo. Wanna find someone's house? You go to the county tax collector's website and enter a name. Bingo!"

"My God, Ed, are you stalking those guys?"

"Nope, I'm just messin' with 'em. By the way, Pritchard's house is right over there." Ed pointed to their left to the part of Key Largo called Pirate's Cove. "That's one of the reasons I wanted to come here, to see if their boat is back. After lunch, we'll go down to the dock and have a look."

"Back? Back from where?" Lenny couldn't believe this.

"I dunno exactly," said Ed. "I just put some gum on their fuel tank breather port. The boat was gonna stall underway maybe ten minutes after they left their dock. It wouldn't damage their boat, mind you. Just messin' with 'em. They'll think it was kids. They have no way of knowin' it was me."

Lenny was horrified. "Ed, I know you guys exchanged words, but that was a crappy thing to do. I've known you for, what, three years and I didn't expect something like this. Are you feeling alright?"

"Lenny, I'm fine. Just relax. It was just a simple prank. Nobody got hurt."

They finished and Lenny paid the check. The men walked downstairs to the small beach and dock. Ed had the binoculars with him. At the end of the dock, Ed looked toward Pirate's Cove. He knew Art's house by its yellow color. He could see Art's boat. It was out of the water and on the lift.

Ed mumbled, "Yup, there she is, high and dry." He turned to his friend and said, "Ya see, Lenny, the boat's fine and they're fine. No harm, no foul."

Lenny didn't speak. He shook his head and walked off the dock to his car and drove home. Ed went home for a nap. After the nap and when *Jenny Girl* was back on the water, Ed planned to pay another visit to Pirate's Cove.

CHAPTER SEVENTEEN

Art and Jackson ate a late breakfast of leftovers from Hobo's. "This Monte Cristo is amazing even the morning after," said Jackson.

"Oh yeah." Art sipped his coffee. "How's the gut today?"

"It bothered me all night," Jackson said. "It wasn't the food. I think it was the notion that someone wants to place us in danger. If they were in front of us, physically, this would be easier. We would just have at it, then it would be over."

"I totally understand, and it bothers me, too. In 'Nam, there were quiet nights when we felt the enemy close by. I hated the anticipation and the uneasy silence. I was hoping they would attack so I could unleash my pent-up energy and my plentiful ammo on them." He paused and added, "Let's get you loaded up with Tums and Pepto Bismol. Okay?"

"Sure. It looks like another nice day. What day is it? I've lost track; apparently there is no calendar in paradise."

"Jackie, it's Thursday, but your point is true: it's easy to lose track of time here." Art paused and asked, "You think you'll be up for another boat ride today? I was thinking we would cruise south of here this afternoon for an hour or two. When the sun is in the west, the sandy bottom over there lights up in the shallow water."

"That sounds perfect, a lazy ride. It's approaching noon now. Okay if we leave around two? I'd like to call Sharon and check in." Jackson drank some Pepto' and he tossed the Tums bottle into the boat bag.

"Sounds good," said Art, "say hi to her for me. Tell her I am taking good care of you."

Jackson showered then dressed. As with everyday, he wore khaki cargo shorts and a polo shirt—the Keys uniform. Today the shirt was white. He looked at his watch. It was 9:45 California time, so he called Sharon. He was delighted to hear her voice.

"Hi Jack, it's great to hear from you. I was beginning to worry a croc' got you."

"Hah, not yet anyway. How are you sweetheart?" He envisioned her pretty, ever-tan face. That and her athletic physique and dyed blond hair convinced most people she was still in her fifties, not seventy.

"Just fine, but I miss your cooking and your snuggles at night." She liked it when Jackson barbequed, and his body heat kept her warm in bed. Perhaps because she was so slim, she always felt chilly.

"Well," he said, "I'll be home Sunday night. I may be tired, so don't expect me to be my usual wacky self." Sharon laughed because Jackson was typically understated and introspective.

"I'll be glad to have you back in any condition. Speaking of which, how is your tummy?"

Jackson fibbed. "It's okay. I'm eating healthy foods and getting plenty of sleep. Art won't let us go carousing at night. He says Key Largo is much too wild for us geezers."

"I'm glad to hear you are taking care of yourself. I'm also glad you'll be seeing the doctor next week to get this thing taken care of. What is Art's place like?" she asked.

"Wonderful, right on the water and furnished like a page in a magazine. It has a view that goes forever, and the weather and water are perfect for boating. Next time, you have to come along. Oh, Art says hi."

"That sounds great. Tell Art I said hello, and thank him for me, for taking care of you. I gotta run, but I am <u>so</u> happy you called. I love you Jack and I miss you."

"I love you too, sweets. Take care. G'bye."

At 2:00 PM, Jackson and Art loaded the boat. After they inspected it for tampering, they motored out of Buttonwood Sound to the Intracoastal Waterway. The sparkling seas were glassy, and the boat ran well. Jackson got more time at the helm. The ride south was, indeed, spectacular. Just as Art had mentioned, the sunlight on the sandy bottom created a luminous, transparent effect. After a slow ride of about seven miles, they shut down the engine near Pigeon Key and went adrift. The scene was exquisite: crystal water, waving palms on the nearby shore, soft lapping of the sea on the hull, and a mild, salty wind.

***

Ed didn't sleep. He was too amped up for a nap. At 2:15, he returned to the small beach at Dockside Grill. Using his binoculars, he could see that Art's boat was gone, out for an afternoon run. He hustled back to his truck and made his way to Pirate's Cove. He pulled into Art's pea rock driveway and parked. Then he quickly climbed out of the truck carrying a fishing knife. Ed approached the white Hyundai in the carport and stabbed the side of the rear left tire. It was hissing as he returned to the truck and drove off. He was in and out in less than a minute.

***

After seventy-five minutes of drifting, the sun and the rhythmic rocking of the boat left Art and Jackson feeling nature-drugged mellow. They slowly made their way home. At the dock, they followed the usual procedure to remove gear, flush the engine, raise the boat, and hose down the hull. The overspray in the light breeze was refreshing in the intense Florida sun. Back in the air conditioned house, Art turned off the power to the boat lift. The discussion turned to dinner.

Art said, "That's the drill here: boating and eating. Can you imagine a better life than that?"

Jackson was missing Sharon. "That would be hard to imagine," he said, "but it would be great if Sharon was also here. It's fun to watch the two of you kidding and teasing."

"Oh yeah. She is a good sport, always great to be around. On our next trip down, she <u>must</u> come along. Or if you like, the two of you can come by yourselves. What's mine is yours, my 'brotha from anotha motha'," Art said.

"Food. We're dressed, and we haven't collapsed into the sofas," said Jackson. "I suggest we surf this momentum and go out for a nice meal, on me."

"Sounds great. I know another good place…"

"Of course you do," Jackson interrupted. It was a compliment.

"It's called Snappers. Great place on the ocean side not far from here. Ready in ten?"

"Sure."

After a bio break, a splash of water to the face and a fresh shirt, they locked up and descended the stairs to the carport. It was well before sunset when Art took the wheel; Jackson was glad to ride shotgun. Their mood was upbeat. It had been a great day. As Art pulled out of the carport onto the pea rock, he felt unusual resistance to the car's movement. Something wasn't right. He stepped out of the Hyundai and looked toward the rear of the vehicle, driver's side. The tire was flat, very flat. He moved closer to look for damage, and the problem was obvious. There was a two-inch gash in the tire's sidewall.

"Son of a bitch," Art yelled, "our sabotage asshole struck again. This tire is ruined. Jackie, would you please change the tire while I ask the neighbors if they saw anyone. I hope we have a decent spare."

"Sure Art, go."

CHAPTER EIGHTEEN

Art didn't notice anyone outside, so he knocked on doors. He was known and liked in the neighborhood. People nearby wanted to help, but he had no luck at the first two houses. At the third house, Jennifer, a sweet woman in her early eighties with thin white hair and deep facial wrinkles, had information.

"Well, I was downstairs doing laundry. I had the window open, the one facing the street. I heard a car pass the house, then I heard its tires crunching on pea rock. You know that sound right?" she asked.

"Absolutely," said Art, "it is unmistakable."

"Art, it was your driveway. I assumed you had a repairman coming over. But the truck didn't stay long at all."

"You said it was a truck. Did you see the color or the make of the truck?"

She said, "I got a good look at it when it came back by. I had heard the crunch again, and I saw the truck drive past. It was red, but I don't know what kind of truck it was. The man driving was on the heavy side. What's going on?" she asked.

"I'm not sure, Jennifer, but this helps a lot," Art said, "thank you. I am glad for neighbors who pay attention to strangers in the area. That's the way we keep each other safe. Thank you again." Art trotted back to his house. Jackson was making progress replacing the tire.

"It's one of those little donut-spares," said Jackson. "I hate these things, but they do the job for a short time. I'm glad it was full of air, solid." When Jackson finished, they went into the house.

While Jackson washed his hands, Art said, "We need a plan to nail this prick. What do we know? At the Lions Club, Tom said his name was Ed and he ran a boat detail service. Do you remember the name?"

"Sorry Art, no. I was a bit amped up by then. Worse case, we could call Tom."

Art looked online. "We'd better leave others outta this. Man, there are a lot of 'em here. How about Bowden Wax and Detailing?"

"No," said Jackson.

"Superior Boat Detailing?"

"No."

Art read six more before saying, "TN Detail Services?"

"That's it!" said Jackson. "What do you want to do, Art?"

"Lemme think a second. We could try to find his office or house, but being inside with him is a bad idea. I'm sure if the late Carlos would speak, he would advise against it. We want Ed outside."

Jackson said, "How about this? We call him and book a boat detailing job. He would never come to this address. He would know it'd be a setup, so we use some other location. Do you have a buddy with a boat in a different part of Key Largo? Ed wouldn't have a clue he was coming to see <u>us</u>."

"Oh Jackie, you are a perverse genius. Sure, let's go see my friend Roger Austin. Good guy, a former Marine with a boat in his front yard. He'll love this."

Art and Jackson drove past the Pilot House restaurant on Seagate Boulevard and parked in front of Roger's house. Roger was there, gave Art a big hug, then introduced himself to Jackson. Roger had the look of a former Marine: crewcut, anvil chin, too-tight Under Armor shirt and bulging biceps. The three went inside. After some banter about tough Rangers and tougher Marines, Art described the incidents with the gum and the slashed tire. Then they formulated a plan for revenge. Roger would book a boat wax appointment with Ed for Friday or Saturday. When Ed arrived to do the job, Art and Jackson would confront Ed. Roger's job was to stand there and look like——Roger. He was <u>loving</u> the idea. Art gave Roger the phone number of TN Detail Services and he dialed. He got an answer.

"Hello, this is Ed."

"Hello sir, my name is Roger. I live in Key Largo. I have an eighteen-foot Action Craft flats boat. She's chalky as hell. How soon could you get a wax job on her?"

"I can get to it early next week. Will that work for you?"

"Frankly no. I'm towing it to West Palm on Monday. Can you find some time sooner? It's a small job, and I'll pay a premium."

After a pause Ed said, "I can squeeze you in tomorrow afternoon around 2:30 if you're willing to pay twenty-five dollars per foot."

"That would be great," said Roger. He winked at Art. "I'm at the corner of Seagate and Madeira, not far from the Pilot House."

Ed said, "Yeah I know where that is. I'll be there at 2:30, have cash for payment. Bye."

Art high-fived Roger and Jackson, then they all celebrated with Guinness Draughts. "So, what is the plan when he arrives tomorrow?" Jackson asked.

Art said, "First we surround him. Roger, you block his access to the truck. Then I am gonna get in his face, make it clear that we either get $300 for the SUV tire right there or we're calling the Sheriff on the spot and filing trespass and vandalism complaints."

"I like that," said Roger. Jackson nodded his agreement.

"I will also say if anything more happens to us or my property, I will mess him up."

"Whoa, Art," said Jackson. "I know you can handle him, but I think we should put ongoing problems in the hands of law enforcement. You were a Sheriff's Officer. Did you want citizens to become vigilantes? I doubt it."

Roger agreed. "Yeah Art, as much as I'd love to help you kick his ass, we would just create more trouble for ourselves."

"Yeah, yeah, I hear you, but give me a little latitude to cause him to trip or something," replied Art.

Roger looked at Jackson. He said, "I don't have a problem if he falls, do you Jackson?"

"Not at all," said Jackson. "I just don't want to see <u>you</u> locked up, Art."

"Alright, it's settled. We'll reconvene here at 2:00 tomorrow," said Art. "See you, Roger, and thanks for making the phone call. You were great."

Jackson and Art departed. They stopped at the Pilot House for some badly needed dinner. They enjoyed their food on the open deck, but they were anxious to get home. It was getting late and neither of them had slept well the night before. They committed to getting a replacement tire for the Hyundai in the morning. In the afternoon they would, metaphorically speaking, smack Mr. Ed.

CHAPTER NINETEEN

It had been a difficult night. Everyone and everything was soaked. Some of the crew were coughing; exposure was taking a toll. From the tiller, Diego asked, "Is everyone alright?"

"Define 'alright'," said Pilar, "that was rough." She and Benito attempted to spread the wet blankets and tarps in the morning sun.

"That was miserable," Benito agreed. Then he said, "Diego, I will take the tiller. You have been up all night." Diego thanked him and moved aside. Then he went to the piss zone of the boat to urinate.

Blanca was sick. She coughed and said, "I hope for sunshine today. I feel so cold, and I am shaking." She was hypothermic. Pilar was sitting next to her, and she put her arms around Blanca. Diego pointed toward Pilar, a gesture of approval.

Diego checked the portable GPS. He knew the others would soon ask about progress. He reported, "We are now 106 miles from Cuba. We moved closer to Florida last night, but the storm slowed us." There was a collective groan.

Yadier sat up, his face was pale and he was angry. He barked at Diego, "Why do you tell us the distance from Cuba? Are you tricking us? Why not tell us how far it is to Florida?"

"I cannot tell you how far it is to the Keys, because I don't know. With the changing wind and current we still don't know exactly where we will make landfall. If I cannot tell you <u>where</u>, I cannot tell you <u>when</u>."

"Now you talk in riddles. Make an estimate, we deserve to know."

Diego said, "We still have at at least another day and a half to go, and that is if we get strong winds. If the winds get lighter, it will take another two days."

"Shit," said Yadier, "you do not know what you are doing. I think you are killing us all." Despite his frustrations Yadier laid back down.

Diego scanned the tangle of bodies on the boat. They looked haggard, wet, dirty, sullen. He feared they couldn't endure two more nights on the chug. Despite his own fatigue, Diego resolved to closely observe each person throughout the day.

Bernardo said, "Diego, come help. Santiago looks bad." Everyone sat up and leaned away to make room for Diego. The doctor tried to speak with Santiago, but he acted sleepy and unresponsive. Diego checked his breathing and pulse; both were very slow.

"He has second stage hypothermia. This can be very dangerous. Bernardo, help me sit him up and put his knees to his chest." Santiago rested his forehead on his knees. "Now Bernardo, please sit close to him, hold him to warm him." Diego hoped the morning sun would also bring Santiago needed warmth.

He spoke to everyone. "From the look of the sky, we will have bright, warm sunshine today. If you are shivering, sit as Santiago is now, huddle your bodies together to retain heat." Everyone scooted closer together.

The day warmed quickly, and Blanca stopped shivering. Santiago still sat with his head down. Bernardo, the strong bear, was doing his best to hold and warm Santiago. Diego distributed the first water of the day. He was relieved the big jug hanging off the boat's stern had not been contaminated during the storm.

Diego said, "Now that it is warmer, everyone help check the boat's condition. Look and reach around you. Are things loose or missing? For example, it is obvious that the posts for the lifelines are down. Some are in the water. We need to gather that rigging and save it.

"Do we still have four oars? Are the added pieces of flotation still secure? If not, re-tie them or ask for help. Benito, the rudder felt a bit loose to me. What do you think?"

"Yes, Diego, it is looser, but it does not feel like it will fall off. It seems okay." Benito added, "I only see two oars. The ones on the left side are gone. The styrofoam flotation is still there."

"Thank you. Yadier, please look in the bilge. I am sure we need to bail more water."

Yadier moved slowly and checked. There was considerable water sloshing around. He said, "You can bail the water. I want to eat first." Diego agreed.

Diego opened the bag of food. The crackers were crushed and wet, but the nuts were still dry. He distributed them to the crew. Because Bernardo had lost interest in fishing, Diego also gave out his bait, the final bits of salami. They still had water on board, but Diego concluded the crew needed vitamins. He opened a can of orange juice with a knife and passed it around.

Before bailing, Diego took another close look at Santiago. "My friend, can you raise your head and speak to me?" Santiago raised his head, but he did not speak. He opened his eyes; they looked vacant. Diego again checked his pulse and breathing. The same.

"Bernardo," he said, "you are doing a very good job. Thank you, and keep it up. How are you feeling?"

"I am okay. I am tired, but I don't feel sick."

"Do you need more food, Bernardo?" Diego whispered. He risked a rebellion, but he knew Bernardo was famished.

"Thanks, Doc' I am fine."

Diego welled up at the big man's compassion. Bernardo had softened after seeing Santiago feeling so sick. Diego smiled and patted Bernardo's knee. Then he moved to Blanca.

"Are you feeling better now? I see you are no longer shaking." He checked her pulse and felt her head. Both seemed normal.

"Yes better, Diego," she said.

"I am very glad."

Diego looked at Yadier and said, "Time for some bailing." Yadier collected the drink glasses. "Pilar, would you help us, please?" Diego asked. "Scooch over to toss the water overboard." She was the only one left on the boat who wasn't recovering or busy.

 Yadier and Diego bumped shoulders when they reached below deck. "*Estúpido*, watch it," said Yadier. Diego didn't react, but he noticed the insult.

With Pilar's help, the men removed many gallons of water. "My back is killing me," said Yadier, "let's stop. This is good enough."

Diego's back was hurting as well. He said, "I agree, Yadier. Thank you for your help. And thank you, Pilar."

With the work done and everyone fed, The boat got quiet. Diego managed some much-needed sleep. Bernardo also slept while still sitting and holding Santiago. Blanca and Pilar huddled nearby. Benito stayed active at the helm as a light southern breeze pushed the rugged boat slowly across the clear, warm Florida Straits. An eight-foot shark swam past the boat, and Benito was the only one to notice. He was troubled by that, but he resolved to not tell anyone. *The crew doesn't need another thing to worry about.*

In the late afternoon, most of the passengers again stirred. Santiago opened his eyes and stretched his body. That woke Bernardo. He said, "Are you feeling better now?"

Santiago nodded and whispered, "Yes. May I have some water?"

Pilar filled a cup and handed it to Bernardo. He held the cup while Santiago drank. Santiago extended his legs and said, "I would like to lie down."

"Sure, let me make room," said Bernardo. He slid to one side, then Santiago laid down. Bernardo removed his soiled white t-shirt, rolled it up, and placed it under Santiago's head. Bernardo then stretched and rubbed his muscles. He hadn't moved in hours.

Everyone else took water as well. Diego spoke. "I am sorry our second meal is late, but I hope everyone got some rest. Benito, I will man the tiller as soon as I eat."

Without looking up, Yadier said, "No, I will."

"Alright, thank you," said Diego.

Diego turned on the GPS to check their progress: 127 miles from Cuba, but a course correction was needed. "Shipmates, we continue to make good progress, now 127 miles miles from Cuba. With luck, we will arrive in the Keys tomorrow evening." The crew gave a cautious cheer. They knew they weren't safe until they stepped on U.S. soil. Even after that their future was uncertain.

"Yadier, steer another fifteen degrees further to the west," Diego said. Yadier didn't respond, but he made the course correction.

An hour later, everyone on the boat became excited when a pod of dolphins swam near. They twice circled the chug. One adult breached as if to say, "Hi neighbor. Having fun?" Blanca felt it was a positive omen, a cause for optimism for the exhausted boaters.

"They will protect us. It is a sign from God," she said. "*Gracias Dios.*" Benito and Blanca made a quick praying motion. Yadier rolled his eyes. The rest did not react.

An hour later the sun sizzled into the sea. In the glorious golden twilight, Diego served more orange juice. Everyone hoped for a night of calm.

CHAPTER TWENTY

"Okay with you if we just hang around this morning, Jackie?" Art wore a yellow t-shirt and blue boxers with anchors on them. The shorts passed for a bathing suit, so they were fine for enjoying the bright morning on the deck. In truth, nobody in the Keys cared anyway.

"Sure, Art. I was thinking the same thing. This afternoon could be quite the event. Plus, this deck is <u>almost</u> like being on a boat." Jackson was very anxious about the planned confrontation with Ed, for good reason. He suspected it would get nasty.

"You'll have to scrounge breakfast again. Sorry. I'm not the most attentive host," confessed Art.

Jackson didn't feel much like eating. "No worries. I'll find something. I saw some bait in the freezer."

They sat quietly on the balcony for a few moments. Next door, a gardener—he appeared to be Latin—turned on his gas-powered weed trimmer. Art said, "Jackie, we had a good conversation about immigration on Tuesday. Mind if we continue that?"

"Fine by me," said Jackson, "but I'd have to figure out where we left off."

Art said, "We were talking about secure borders or unsecure borders. I think we need secure borders. Those who want to come here should go through the legal process, not break the law."

"That might make sense if the 'legal process' wasn't so screwed up and inconsistently applied. Hell, it takes three-to-four years to work through all that."

"So what's the problem with that?" asked Art. "A lot of people <u>do</u> invest the required time to do the right thing. How can open borders be fair to them?"

Jackson said, "Your 'right thing' comment, that is a judgement you make, not me. That aside, think of rainwater flowing down a bank in a forest. That water is going to find the easiest route to get down that hill. It's like that with people: they will look for the easiest or most productive way to a solution. It's human nature. For, say, Cubans, that means crossing the Florida Straits in a few days versus dealing with haphazard governmental bureaucracy for four years."

"So, it's right because it's expedient?" asked Art. "Maybe it's expedient for me to just take your money rather than earning my own. Judge Judy isn't going to go for that argument."

"Of course not, but immigration is more abstract. It's core rests in the observance of human rights. Are borders more important than, say, the rights of people fleeing oppression? It can be even simpler than that. People should have the right to seek a better life."

"Gotcha back, Jackie," Art said. "You said 'people should have the right.' That's a value statement on your part. But to respond to your point, I have no quibble about the right for people to seek a better life, but that doesn't necessarily translate to an open-border policy. I would say to them 'Go seek your better life, but respect our ability to decide if it's going to be on our land'."

"Our beloved symbol of freedom, our Lady Liberty says, 'Give me your tired, your poor, your huddled masses yearning to breathe free.' We have always welcomed foreigners. As I said previously, we were built as a nation mostly by immigrants," said Jackson.

"And for sixty years most of them went through a <u>process</u> at Ellis Island just a half-mile from the Statue of Liberty. As we both know, there was a time when immigrants who arrived in the Bay Area spent a long time in processing at Angel Island. This notion isn't new, Jackie."

"True, but it is flawed. The places you just named are closed, considered to be relics of a myoptic, racist past."

"Well Jackie, we got to the 'R-word.' I think that's a good place to stop. I'm not denying anything you said. I just think the word 'racist' is thrown around way too loosely these days. Shit, if I don't like Mexican food, I must be a racist."

"That's a valid point. 'Racist' is so often used unfairly or improperly it's become trite. I agree, this is a good place to stop. Good talk, Art."

Art responded with a thumbs up and looked Jackson directly in the eyes and said, "Jackson, you <u>do</u> know this is about policy, right? I have nothing against Mexicans, Canadians, Latvians, Martians, whomever."

"Art, I know you. This isn't some kind of hate thing with you."

"Good. Now, in spite of this wonderful view and great conversation, I am really hungry. Are you okay if we go for an early lunch?"

"But you said there were plenty of bait fish in the freezer," said Jackson. "I saw them. Yum." Art laughed.

"With all this talk of immigration, I am thinking about a Cuban Sandwich. There is a place nearby named Denny's that makes good ones," said Art.

"Really. You wanna go to Denny's." It wasn't a question.

"No wait, mine is an independent place, not the Denny's chain nobody visits on purpose. They just end up there for lack of a better option," Art quipped.

"Cuban food: I am suspecting it is spicy. Not sure my belly is interested."

Art said, "Nope. A Cuban Sandwich is ham, pork shoulder and Mex' cheese on a soft Mexican roll. There is a side sauce called *Mojo* that adds spice, but it is optional. Oh, and the sandwich is pressed on a griddle to give the bread a bit of crunch. You will like it. I'll bet a bottle of Tums on it."

"Alright Art. I'm hungry and it sounds pretty good. We'll leave in, what, fifteen minutes? I'm not sure the Cubans want to see your boxers." Art flashed another thumbs up.

They dressed, then they drove seven minutes and parked. The SUV's inflated donut still served heroically as the back-left tire. As they exited the car, Art said, "I gotta remember to get a new tire before we return this beast at the airport."

Outside the eatery, Jackson looked up at the huge red sign and said, "You were right; Denny's Latin Cafe looks nothing like the Denny's of last resort." Inside it looked even less like the familiar chain. There were murals of Cuban beaches and landmarks plus colorful landscape paintings. The brightly colored decor compensated for the lack of windows.

"Hi Rosa," said Art, "this *gringo* is my friend Jackson." Art wasn't really sure if Cubans used the word *gringo*.

Rosa shouted, "Welcome *Jacksone*. We are glad you are here. Please sit. Some beer for you?" It was 11:00 AM.

Art said, "No thanks, Rosa. How about a couple *Jarritos*? Jackie, lime, fruit punch or mandarin?"

"Mandarin for me, thanks," said Jackson. *Jarritos* were also popular in California; they were tasty Mexican sodas with real sugar, not corn syrup.

They settled into a booth. "Great place, eh Jackie?"

Jackson agreed. "The place has character, but you're <u>sure</u> the food won't involve flames?"

"No Jackie, you'll be fine."

Rosa asked for their order. She was a tiny woman with a weathered face. She wore a faded blue print dress with lace on the sleeves and hem; her ancient tan shoes were made of woven hemp.

Jackson hadn't looked at the menu, but Art asked to order. He told Rosa, "*Amiga Rosa*, one Cuban Sandwich and one *Media Noche*. Okay?" She smiled and returned to the kitchen.

Jackson asked, "What's the other sandwich?"

"*Media Noche* means 'midnight' but I'm not sure what that has to do with the sandwich. It has the same ingredients as a Cuban, but the bread is a bit lighter with a slightly different taste. Both are excellent."

They reflected on the week. Art said, "Jackie, this has been a fun week and a stressful week. This nonsense with Crazy Ed is unusual. I've never experienced anything like it. You've seen how we're treated in restaurants and by others like Roger? The locals are really, really, good people, rock solid. This Ed-dude is the exception. He has serious issues. I guess there are a few loonies everywhere."

Jackson said, "I get it, Art. Not to sound all 'sixties' on you, but Key Largo has a nice vibe. It feels like a big boating club without the blazers. I can see why you like it so much."

"And the food, it's excellent and cheap. Thanks for paying, by the way, and please forget my failures with our non-breakfasts. I have been a lazy host. Next time it's eggs benedict served with a chilled Kir Royale every morning, scout's honor." Art held up his right hand.

"We've done just fine. My cargo shorts feel tighter."

Their food arrived promptly; the browned sandwiches were cut in half. Art asked, "You wanna try a half of each or pick just one? As I said, they are very similar."

"Let's mix it up. They both look very good."

They were silent while they ate. Rosa checked on them, and she brought a second round of *Jarritos*. When they finished the sandwiches, Rosa asked about dessert. The choices were *flan* and *churros*. Jackson and Art declined. After Jackson paid they said goodbye to Rosa.

On the drive home, Jackson said, "That was great, Art. Whew, I'm stuffed. You were right about the sandwiches, very tasty. Thanks."

"Thank you. Yet another free meal for me." Art's voice turned more serious. "We have ninety minutes before going to Roger's place. I'll text him to find out if there are any changes to the schedule. Meanwhile, why don't you relax on the balcony, enjoy this nice break."

"Sounds good." His stomach was in earthquake mode. He ate too much and he was stressing about the plan for the afternoon. He gulped some Pepto' and stretched out on the balcony. After fifteen minutes, Art opened the slider to confirm that the plans remained firm. He closed the slider and stayed inside to "Muck with some paperwork," he'd said.

When it was approaching 2:00 PM, they locked up and drove to Roger's. Art reminded himself again to get a new tire.

CHAPTER TWENTY-ONE

Ed finished his first contract of the day. "Pablo, you were a great help today, and that was a bitch of a job. Beside it bein' hot, the hull on that scow had hair longer than Cher's. Here's your share." Ed handed his worker Pablo one-fourth of the earnings, $130.

"Much appreciated, thanks, Ed. Call me again anytime."

The men left in separate vehicles. Ed didn't need help with his afternoon appointment, so he hadn't mentioned it to Pablo. Ed drove through Wendy's for some lunch. He shoved down a massive burger and a chocolate shake before finishing the fifteen-minute drive home. Inside, he pulled off his sweat-soaked shirt, and he collapsed into his leather lounger. He turned on the television and found an episode of Dateline. Within twenty minutes he was asleep.

At 2:15 he woke up. It took a few seconds for him to get oriented. He remembered his afternoon boat-wax gig, then he looked at his watch. "Holy shit," he said. He found his note with the customer's address on his cluttered kitchen table. He retrieved his sweaty shirt from the floor and bolted out the door. In ten minutes Ed was at the jobsite on Seagate Boulevard. His scribbled note said the customer had an eighteen-foot Action Sport flats boat; it was there in the driveway. Ed climbed out of his truck and pulled his detailing gear and supplies from the back. Then he walked toward the customer's boat.

Three men came out the front door. They encircled Ed. At first he didn't recognize the Californians. When he did, he said, "What are you assholes doing here? This ain't your boat, is it?"

"It's mine," said Roger. As planned, Roger stood between Ed and his red truck. Roger wore no shirt, and he looked fierce.

Ed said, "So am I waxing it or not?"

Art stepped closer—he towered over Ed—and he said, "No, you're here to explain the damage to my SUV tire and the gum on my boat."

"What're you talking about? I didn't do anything. I'm outta here." Ed turned toward his truck.

Roger stepped in front of him and said firmly, "No, you're not. Sit down." When Ed tried to move around him, Roger clutched Ed's arm and said, louder this time, "Sit your fat ass down!"

Ed sat on the searing pea rock. He was sweating, and he pursed his lips. He realized this was serious.

Art knelt close to Ed and said, "Now I want you to extend your legs and cross your ankles. Lock your hands behind your head."

Ed complied then he asked, "What is this, a shakedown? Am I on 'Live PD'?"

"Shut up. I'll tell you in a minute. First, because we are in the abundantly-armed Keys, I'm gonna check you for weapons." Art patted him down; back, hips, chest. Then he emptied Ed's pockets. Art placed Ed's wallet, keys, Wendy's coupons and medication bottle on the pea rock.

Jackson was impressed. Art's presence was intimidating as hell, and he had complete control of the situation using a professional and firm approach. It was clear he had immobilized suspected perps hundreds of times.

"Okay, now that you got to fondle me, what do you want?" said Ed.

Art looked directly into Ed's eyes. "You messed with my boat and you slashed my tire. You're giving me $300 for my replacement tire."

Ed defiantly said, "I don't owe you shit."

Art's voice was louder this time. "Did I mumble or speak in a foreign language? You are giving me $300 right now."

"Look, I can see you're pissed, but I can't spare $300. I have a sick daughter who depends on me."

Art got within two inches of Ed's face. He gritted his teeth and with scorching conviction Art said, "You're confusing me with someone who gives a shit. We have proof that you are guilty of trespassing and vandalism. Give me the money now or Thor, Rambo and I are gonna stuff you into my damaged SUV and present you, bleeding profusely, to the Sheriff. I promise, I'm not gonna ask again."

"Okay, okay. I'll give you the money. I have cash in my wallet."

Art lowered his voice and he spoke deliberately. "So, you are giving me permission to open your wallet and take out $300, right?" Ed nodded.

"Not good enough," said Art. "I want you to confirm that loud enough so my brothers hear it very clearly. Now speak up, Eddie."

Ed spoke loudly. His voice cracked from nerves. "Yes, I want you to take $300 from my wallet. It is yours."

Art turned to retrieve the wallet. He opened it, pulled out the cash, and he counted out $300. He put it in his pocket. Art put the rest of the cash back in the wallet and placed it on the ground in front of Ed. He moved Ed's other possessions to the same spot. Then he looked Ed again in the eyes.

Art said, "Look, you steaming piece of shit, we are square now, but I am still very unhappy; you messed up my friend's vacation. When I finish talking, you're taking your stuff and getting into that truck. Then you are driving away. I never wanna see you again. If my new security cameras see you near my house again, either I or my shotgun-loving neighbor is gonna hunt you and blow a new hole in your ass. You live on Abaco Road, right? Yeah. Now go."

Ed gathered his belongings and stood. His face was flushed and expressionless. Although his knees were weak, he walked briskly to his truck. He started it and drove away without looking back. Because of the heat, the three went back into Roger's house. Like before, he served up a round of Guinness Draughts.

Art said casually, "Well, I expect that's the last we'll see of that little prick."

"Good job, Art. That all went as planned," said Roger.

Jackson couldn't believe how understated the others were, but he responded similarly. "Yeah, Art. You certainly solved the problem. Good job." *Oh my God, did I just participate in revenge, extortion, or was it karma? Art was masterful.*

Roger said, "When you mentioned the street he lives on, he freaked out. I thought he was gonna piss himself."

"How did you know he lived on Abaco Road, Art?" asked Jackson.

"I had a real estate friend check public records while you relaxed on the deck after lunch. I thought it would help drive home my message, so to speak."

Art and Jackson finished their beers. They thanked Roger for his help, then headed home in the limping Hyundai. Jackson said to Art, "I am glad you got the money to replace the tire, but I have a question. Would the law consider that little confrontation extortion or maybe a mugging?"

Art pursed his lips, nodded and said, "Yeah, that was a shakedown, muscle for money. Not an admirable thing to do. We're here for only a week, so I didn't have time to go through the legal process to get my money back. But expediency is not a legitimate excuse."

"Hey," said Jackson, "I'm not judging you. You didn't notice me objecting at the time. Just asking a question."

"Oh I know, Jackie, and it's a fair question. I hope you know I didn't do shit like that when I was a cop or a Sheriff's Officer. It was all on the up and up. I <u>enjoyed</u> taking dickheads like Ed to the station."

"Enough said, my friend," said Jackson.

On the way home, they stopped at Mrs. Mac's for an early dinner. Jackson's stomach was still feeling the tension, so he ate very little. Art celebrated with a piece of baked snapper, fries, coleslaw, and a glass of chardonnay. He topped it off with a slice of Key Lime Pie. This time their meal at Mrs. Mac's went uninterrupted.

CHAPTER TWENTY-TWO

It had been a rough, miserable night and the water jug had been sheared off the chug by the relentless, turbulent sea. Pilar and Santiago were still asleep, but the rest were awake and somber. "I took second shift at the tiller," said Benito, "and I didn't notice the big water jug was missing. I felt the boat closer to the seawater surface like now, but I didn't pay attention to the water jug. Maybe it got loose then. I was focused on holding our course."

Blanca agreed with her husband. "We were bouncing like corks, but at least it didn't rain. We lost our water?" She looked terrified.

"We have some other water in small bottles plus juice and milk. Let's not panic," said Diego. He looked at Yadier and said, "Yadier, you were steering before Benito. Do you remember seeing the water jug still attached?"

"I don't know. I only remember a noise under the deck, then the boat sorta sank a bit. What does it matter now? The boat is still floating." Yadier added, "Diego, check our progress. We had a lot of wind. Maybe we are very close to Florida now."

While Diego waited for the GPS to boot up, he said, "The winds were swirling all night. It must have been hard for both of you on the tiller." From the stern, Benito nodded his agreement; Yadier didn't react. "I will relieve you very soon," said Diego.

Diego was disappointed with the GPS reading. "We are 139 miles from Cuba." The exhausted, angry group protested loudly.

"We went only twelve miles overnight? How can that be?" said Benito.

Pilar was awakened by Benito's voice. "What is wrong?" she asked.

Yadier explained the problem to Pilar then he said, "This is bullshit. Benito, did you even steer?"

"Of course," spat Benito. "When I took over, we were sailing south. You screwed up."

"You idiots, we are going to die out here," shrieked Pilar.

"Shut up, bitch," Yadier yelled, "you slept all night. You can steer tonight."

Bernardo jumped in, but his concern was hunger. "Diego, bring out the goddam food, I am dying here."

"Shut your mouths everybody!" shouted Diego. Even he was losing patience. "We are all tired and hungry. I will give out food and drink."

He passed out the last of the nuts to his shipmates, then he poured orange juice from the last can. Diego also offered sweet condensed milk, but no one was interested. After that, he tried to wake Santiago to feed him. Santiago was unresponsive. Everyone watched as Diego checked Santiago's breathing and his pulse.

Diego looked up. The group was quiet. "He is gone."

A collective gasp filled the boat. Blanca sobbed, and everyone cried. Benito said softly, "*Dios mio.*"

"I am glad I got to hold him yesterday," said Bernardo. Then he broke down.

"I can't believe it," said Benito. "Poor man."

"What do we do now, Diego. I mean…" Pilar's voice trailed off as she put her hand over her mouth.

Diego said, "We will place his body in the sea. Originally, we all came from the sea. It is the right thing to do, but I will need your help."

They wrapped Santiago's small body in his blanket. Diego searched for something to add weight to the body, but he found nothing. They wrapped the blanket with pieces of rope previously cut from the ruined lifelines. Santiago's bundled body was laid on the downwind side of the deck.

Diego asked, "Does anyone want to say something?" They were all groggy and shocked. Blanca was still crying; Benito did his best to comfort her.

Bernardo said, "Santiago, you were a good man, and I will miss you."

"Rest in peace, *amigo*," said Yadier. Others in the group said something similar. Benito and Blanca crossed themselves.

Diego spoke last. "It was an honor to know you, Santiago. You were a man of dignity and kindness. I am sad that you left us, but I pray you will enjoy everlasting life in heaven." After a pause, he said to Bernardo, "Please help me commit our friend to the sea."

The two men placed him in the warm water. Santiago's body floated away on the shining, silver surface.

"That was very sad," said Blanca.

"Yes, and Santiago's passing is in great contrast with this beautiful, bright day," said Pilar. "I feel clouds in my heart."

"I agree totally, such an otherwise wonderful day," said Diego. "But now I must direct our attention to the boat."

Blanca panicked again. "Oh my God, are we sinking?"

"I am not sure, but the boat certainly has a problem," said Diego. "We will figure it out together." He turned his head and said, "Yadier, would you please check the bilge?"

"You do it. I was up half the night," said Yadier.

"Yadier, you are such a jackass," said Benito, "you're gonna be the next one tossed off the boat."

Pilar shouted, "You are assholes. Just shut up, both of you. We are all going to die anyway because you steered the boat back toward Cuba."

Diego tried to distract the group and get Benito off the tiller; he was falling asleep. "Bernardo, would you please steer the boat. It is my turn on the tiller, but I want to focus on these problems," he said.

Bernardo was not happy, but he slid over to the tiller. There was very little wind and the sail hung limp. For the moment, steering didn't accomplish much.

Diego looked into the bilge. The seawater was only twenty inches below the deck. Through the clear water, he could see that a plank had become detached from the hull. Besides leaving a gaping hole, the hanging board was slowing their progress. Most of the cans of condensed milk were still in the bilge. Diego reported to the group.

"We have a breach in the hull. That is why the boat is lower in the water. However, the styrofoam and sealed jugs below are keeping us afloat and they will continue to do so."

Some of the weary crew sighed; a couple nodded. Yadier said, "No more bailing for me. *Bueno!*"

"But we still have a problem," cautioned Diego. "The piece of wood that came loose is slowing us down. Although we don't have tools, the water is calm enough to try to repair it."

During Diego's report, Pilar pulled down her shorts and leaned her butt over the edge of the boat to urinate. All potty protocols had been abandoned. Nobody seemed to care.

Diego continued. "As I said, we have no tools, but if someone could get into the water and swim down there and push the board up through the hull, that would help reduce the drag on the boat. I can try it unless someone else prefers to do it." There was silence.

"Okay, I will do it," said Diego. While still seated, he pulled off his shirt and his pants. When he extended his legs he accidentally kicked Benito, who was sleeping.

Benito wiped his face with both hands and muttered, "What is happening?"

Diego apologized and said, "The sea is calm. I am going into the water to fix a leak."

Benito nodded passively, but when Diego stood and prepared to jump overboard, Benito shouted, "No, stop!" The whole crew was startled.

Diego paused and stared at him curiously. Benito said, "I saw a large shark yesterday. You were all sleeping, and I decided not to tell you."

While others onboard expressed alarm, Diego sat down on the boat and silently looked at the deck. After a moment he directed his eyes to Benito. "My friend, thank you for telling me. Maybe today the sharks are not hungry, but I would rather not tempt them."

Benito responded, "Me neither."

CHAPTER TWENTY-THREE

"Now we know, everyone. No swimming or getting in the water to go to the toilet," said Diego. He needn't have said anything; the crewmembers were scanning the water for more predators.

Diego spoke softly, "It will take us forever to get Florida with that board hanging in the water. How do we fix it?"

"I have an idea," said Bernardo. He was depressed and sleepy, but for the moment he spoke with clarity. "If we have any rope left, we could go into the water under the deck and put a loop around the board sticking out below the boat. Then we could pull it back up against the boat. What do you think, doc?"

Some of the crew hadn't listened. A couple others loudly rejected the idea and ridiculed Bernardo. They were too fatigued to follow along. Diego said, "Bernardo, that is a brilliant idea. I hope we have some rope left." Benito found a piece under the pile of blankets.

"Bernardo," said Diego, "we have no wind, so leave the tiller and come help me. You have long arms. We can do this."

Diego tied a loop in the rope. Each man was too large to get his shoulder or torso into the opening in the deck. Bernardo tried reaching to the bottom of the boat, but it was too far. He tried dangling the rope into the flooded boat, but its weight wasn't sufficient to carry the loop to the bottom. Diego thought about putting weights on the rope, but they couldn't find anything suitable. Diego motioned for Pilar to join them. She was the smallest person on the boat. Although she was weary, she was willing to help. Diego asked her to try reaching below the boat's deck. She was able to get her shoulders below. Bernardo and Diego looked at each other; they knew she was part of the solution.

"Pilar, you can help fix the boat." She was confused, but Diego continued. "Down under the boat there is a board sticking out by fourteen inches. Take a look, you can see it." She could see the bent board and the opening it created.

Diego continued. "That board is slowing down the boat. We would like you to put this loop around it. After that, we will pull on the rope to bring the board against the bottom of the boat. That will help us go faster."

"Wait, which board is fourteen inches long?" she asked. Pilar was very tired. Diego explained it again.

"So how do I get the rope around the board? I can't swim down there, and I am <u>not</u> jumping off the boat and fighting sharks, but I will do whatever else you need." Pilar was a trooper.

Diego explained, "Bernardo is going to hold you upside down and lower you below the deck far enough for you to put this loop over the end of the board. I will hold the other end of the rope. Your head will be underwater, so you will have to hold your breath. It should take only fifteen seconds, then Bernardo will pull you up." Diego paused, then he asked, "Pilar, can you do this?"

Pilar looked below deck for a few seconds, then she said, "Okay, yes."

Diego and Bernardo were delighted, but Pilar's safety had to be considered. Diego asked, "Are you right handed?" Pilar nodded. "Okay, you will hold the rope's loop in your right hand. I want you to keep your left hand at your side where I can see it. If you need for Bernardo to lift your head out of the water, make a fist. Show me a fist with your left hand." She curled her hand into a fist. "Excellent. That is your signal for us to pull your head out of the water. Is that clear?"

"Yes, I understand. If I make a fist, Big Bernardo will pull me up."

They practiced a few times until Pilar and Bernardo were ready. On Diego's signal, Bernardo dunked Pilar. Diego held the other end of the rope. Pilar's upper body wiggled as she manipulated the rope with her right arm. She signalled with a fist, and Bernardo pulled her up immediately. Pilar sat on the deck and wiped her face. She still had the loop in her hand.

"I was close," she said, "but I need to be lowered further. Then it will work. Let me catch my breath, and we can try again."

Diego patted her on the shoulder and said, "Take your time. No rush."

After a few minutes, Pilar and Bernardo made another try. This time Bernardo put her lower in the boat. Again there was wiggling as Pilar reached for the board. Soon after, her left fist indicated she needed to surface. Bernardo lifted her, she didn't have the loop in her hand.

Pilar was excited as she wiped the water from her face. "It worked," she said. The three laughed, and Bernardo gave her a bear hug.

"Thank you so much, Pilar," said Diego. "I think you are part mermaid."

Pilar smiled and said, "After days in the sun, that water felt wonderful. Maybe everyone should get a turn."

Diego firmly grasped the rope that was now tied around the loose plank. He pulled on it to raise the detached plank, but it moved only slightly. After three more tries, the board moved closer to the hull, but when pressure was released, it sprung back to its obstructive position. Diego needed to take a break.

"Let me try," said Bernardo. He placed his feet against the opposite side of the deck's opening and tugged mightily on the rope.

Diego peered into the bilge hoping for progress. "You got it up to the hull, Bernardo, now release the line," he said.

"Okay," said Bernardo as he relaxed the line. The wayward plank sprung back below the hull, though not as far as it was before.

Diego said, "Maybe you can pull the board back up again then I can tie it to the decking. That would keep it from being a significant drag on the boat. We know we can't stop the leak."

Bernardo was tired of the process. "Maybe we just leave it alone, boss. The boat is still floating, and I am out of gas," he said. He leaned to his left and plopped on the deck.

"My friend," said Diego, "the boat is floating, that is true. Our problem is the plank slowing the boat. The rest don't know it yet, but we finished the food this morning. Look around you. We are already weak, the boat is breaking, and this morning we have no wind. Somehow we must reach Florida tomorrow or I fear we won't make it at all. Bernardo," he pleaded, "let's give it another shot."

Bernardo sighed, then he sat up. "Okay, Diego," he said, "but if we make it to Florida, you owe me 100 US."

"Of course, my friend, I promise," said Diego. *Right now I would promise $10,000 and I would find a way to pay it.*

Bernardo took the rope from Diego. He sat quietly for a moment with his feet propped across the opening. He took a deep breath and hauled mightily on the rope; he gritted his teeth and the blood vessels in his neck stood out. Diego feared the rope would break. After a few seconds of straining, the tension on the rope released, and Bernardo fell backwards onto Yadier. Diego had been looking into the bilge, and he got splashed with water. His instinctive recoil nearly caused him to fall overboard. Both men righted themselves and peered into the bilge.

Bernardo said, "How did that happen?" The board had been pulled between the adjacent boards and was now resting atop them <u>inside</u> the bilge.

Diego said, "I saw the board against the opening, then it burst through and we both fell backward. Maybe the wood is soft from the water." He really didn't know.

Bernardo still held the rope. He pulled the rest from the water and handed it to Diego. The loop was intact. Bernardo said, "I am going to sleep now. You owe me 100 US." He laid down on the damp deck.

"You earned it big man, thank you."

CHAPTER TWENTY-FOUR

There was no wind. After the repair, the chug continued to drift in the baking afternoon sun. The temperature was approaching 100 degrees, and the motionless crewmembers were strewn across the deck like discarded mannequins. Diego sat up and tried to rally the group. "Everyone, we must keep pushing ourselves." No one responded. "We have no wind, but we have oars. We have to keep moving toward Florida or we will die."

"It is too hot. Shut up and let us sleep, Diego," said Yadier.

Bernardo said, "Not working now. Too tired. Tonight we will have wind." The rest only moaned.

Diego decided to bribe them. "People," he said, "it is time for liquids. Sit up and I will serve you."

Benito sat up, so did Pilar. Both were sweating profusely. Without success, the two tried to motivate others near them. Diego found the last water bottle, and he shared sips with Pilar and Benito.

Benito was very concerned about his wife Blanca. Being exhausted and dehydrated himself, he described her behavior as best he could. "She seems awake and moves her eyes. Nothing when I talk to her.

Today she saw colorful parakeets flying. Sometimes she,"—Benito made a ducking motion—"from the birds. She is so hot. You see, I am trying to shade her from the sun."

"You are doing the right thing," said Diego. He was glad Benito took some water. Diego created a bit of shade also for Benito. Then Diego tried getting Blanca to drink. She sipped a little of the tepid water. She turned away. Her stress and the miserable conditions were causing her hallucinations. For the first time Diego believed they were not going to make it. He laid on the deck and went to sleep.

The bouncing and rocking of the boat woke him. It was nearly sunset, and the wind had picked up. He crawled over Yadier and Benito to reach the tiller. It was unattended and jerking violently; Diego was thankful it hadn't fallen off. Instinctively, he steered northwest. He switched on the GPS and adjusted to a more precise heading. During that day, the boat had traveled as much to the east as they had north. They were 155 miles from Cuba but still not close to land. However, the brisk wind was cause for hope.

CHAPTER TWENTY-FIVE

"Well Jackie, it's your last day in paradise. I ordered up a gorgeous Saturday for you. What's your pleasure: the Key Largo Public Library, the bird sanctuary, or maybe some boating on that pristine, glassy water out there?"

"I'll have to think about it. Done: boating!" said Jackson.

"Good answer. The winds are supposed to be calm all day. We still need to get you out on the ocean side of Key Largo. You will love it."

Jackson asked, "When do you want to head out?"

"Well, I think we should have a legitimate meal this morning, no more leftovers. We could boat to Sundowners—you saw it next to Jimmy Johnson's—then we could take a second shot at going through the Adams Cut. I don't expect boat problems now that Mr. Ed is home with his tail between his legs."

"Perfect. So we leave at, say, 10:45?"

"Sure. That gives us time to clean up and prep the boat," said Art.

Shortly after 10:30, they loaded the usual gear, fired up *Jenny Girl* and let her run for a few minutes to verify the engine was operating and cooling properly. With Jackson at the helm, they made their way leisurely to Blackwater Sound. Jackson approached the restaurant slowly, and he put the boat gently against the restaurant's dock. Art secured the lines. In a few minutes they were seated under an umbrella at Sundowners.

"I gotta say, Art, this is a fabulous place, the whole Key Largo area. Except for wanting to be with Sharon and needing to see my doctor back home, I hate to leave."

"So how is your gut today? You seem okay," said Art.

"To be honest, I feel like I swallowed a cactus," Jackson said. "I think it's because my stomach is empty. Eating something benign should help, and I'm glad we have a lazy day ahead."

"Yup, a nice little cruise. Oh, we'd better decide on lunch," said Art, "here comes our server. And Jackie, I'm buying today. No arguments."

"Thanks, Art. I'm having the lobster mac and cheese and a glass of water. I figure those are the most bland things on the menu. I'm also a cheap date."

Ted, their server, approached and took their orders. Art got barbecue ribs and a Miller Lite. While waiting for their meals, Art shared some Keys trivia with Jackson.

"Early in the week, I mentioned the Florida Straits on the ocean side. That separates us from Cuba and the rest of the Caribbean. After we go through the cut, we will be in a protected area. It's called John Pennekamp Coral Reef State Park. It's a popular dive site that is quite famous."

"An aquatic state park. That's clever. How big is it?" asked Jackson.

"I'd say roughly twenty-five miles along the coast and about two and a half miles offshore. The larger coral reef—Pennekamp is a small part of that—extends about six miles out. It is very shallow, so it is a diver's heaven.

"After that, it drops off to hundreds of feet. That's where folks catch the big fish like dolphin. I don't mean Flipper; it's a fish for eating. On a menu, just as you saw here, you will often see it listed as Mahi. That's to keep the tourists from freaking out."

Their food and drink arrived. Jackson said, "Very interesting. I'm getting more excited."

"That big reef has a lot of history. For centuries and before charts of this area were accurate, pirate vessels and merchant ships from all over Europe sailed these waters. Hundreds of them crashed on the reef and spilled their cargos along the ocean floor. Perhaps the most famous ship was the *Atocha*." Jackson was loving the history lesson.

"Her full name was *Nuestra Senora de Atocha*," Art said. "In 1622, she was part of a Spanish fleet of twenty-eight ships carrying precious metals, coins and jewels from Cuba to Spain. A hurricane hit the fleet, and eight of the ships wrecked on the reef, including *Atocha*. Hundreds of sailors died. Treasure estimated to be worth $450 million from just that one ship rested on the seafloor for nearly 400 years.

"A persistent guy named Mel Fisher searched for sixteen years until he found it in 1985. He's gone now, but his company's still recovering artifacts from that ship and others. There's even a Mel Fisher museum in Key West with *Atocha* items for sale, although any jewelry store in the Keys will have *Atocha* silver coins for sale. They are not cheap, but they are legitimate pieces of history."

Jackson said, "What a great story, real shipwrecks and treasure. I am fascinated by nautical history. Thanks for telling me all that."

"My pleasure, Jackie. I thought you might like to know the reef has a rich history, no pun intended. There are lots of wrecks out there and even some old crashed aircraft. We need to hustle out there; this is such a nice day."

Art paid the check, and they boarded *Jenny Girl*. After leaving Sundowners, Art motored five minutes and they could see an opening ahead on the left.

"Is that the Adams Cut?" asked Jackson.

"Yes," said Art. "That will take us to the ocean side."

After passing a marker, they turned left into the cut. This was different from going between the mangroves. It was a concrete canal that sliced through a residential part of Key Largo. At a level above their heads, houses and boats on lifts lined the canal. They motored under Highway 1, and very soon they entered Largo Sound, which resembled a lake. They crossed the sound, then Art directed the boat south through a maze of narrow passages between mangroves.

After ten minutes, Jackson and Art were in open water. It was slightly rougher than on the bay side, so Art pointed the boat to the northeast, taking the chop on the port bow.

"This is spectacular," said Jackson. "I can see forever—endless crystalline water, the lighthouses that mark the edge of the coral reef, even massive tankers in the deep water plowing their way north."

CHAPTER TWENTY-SIX

Ed Melnik woke up cranky from the previous day's ambush. Although he had messed with the big guy's boat and slashed his SUV tire, Ed felt like he'd been held up. Being forced to hand over $300 was excessive, he believed. Ed could get an adequate used tire at B&B for a song. However, he did not want to contact the Sheriff to complain. That would go sideways fast. Ed was looking for a nice day on the water with Lenny. He called to confirm their meeting time.

"Lenzo, this is Ed. What time are we gonna run your boat today?"

"Hi Ed. Looks like we have a really good day. What time do you want to leave my place?"

"How about I come over at 12:30?" said Ed.

"Sure, that works. I'll have *Tinkerbell* ready to go."

"Good. See you then." Ed hung up.

Ed ran errands, stopping at the Arby's near K-Mart for a roast beef sandwich. He liked the food and the deep sound of their spokesperson saying, "We've got the meats." Sometimes around women at bars, Ed would imitate the familiar commercial by pointing to his crotch and saying, "We've got the meats." The women were repulsed but Ed didn't notice.

By the time he finished his beef and cheddar sandwich, it was 12:15 and time to hustle over to Lenny's place on Bahama Avenue—a small, beige cinder block house with direct canal access to the Florida Straits.

Lenny's boat was in the water behind the house, so Ed didn't bother knocking on the door. "Hi Lenny. The Mako looks great. I love that powerful Yam' 200," he said.

"Thanks Ed, it's a good boat and motor, and I am really happy everything still functions: the trim tabs, VHF radio and the Garmin color GPS. Given what I paid, it has worked out swell."

Ed winced at the term "swell" as he stepped aboard and placed his boat bag on the aft deck. "Ed, you do know *Tinkerbell* is a fairy, right?"

"Yes, yes, Ed. You mention that every trip, and each time I explain that Helen had to name the boat or she would have gotten a kitchen remodel instead. So, it was *Tinkerbell* or Bosch appliances."

"Yeah I know, Len. I just like pullin' your chain."

Lenny started the engine, then Ed released the dock lines and pushed off the seawall. As they slid through the canals to open water, Ed said, "Hey skipper, the conditions are so good, you okay if we stay on the ocean side today? Maybe we could buzz out to the Carysfort Lighthouse."

"Sure. I always enjoy going out there and beyond the reef. On a flat day like this, we can cruise that deep water without pounding the boat."

Ed said sarcastically, "We must not beat up *Tinkerbell*. The fairy-boat might get hurt." Lenny did not respond. As they headed into open water, he was busy activating the GPS and the VHF radio.

170

CHAPTER TWENTY-SEVEN

The chug smelled of vomit, feces and urine. The filthy, depleted immigrants moved only involuntarily with the sea's relentless, random motion. Their skin was burnt and blistered. As the welcome sun rose higher in the east, the man at the tiller feared he was the only one still alive.

Diego was dead tired himself after steering the half-submerged boat overnight in stiff winds. But his determination paid off. "We are only nine miles from Key Largo," he announced to the listless crew. His voice was raspy from fatigue and exposure. "We are going to make it. Everybody, please hold on for a couple more hours."

Yadier raised a hand, perhaps as a salute. "Yes, good morning, Yadier," said Deigo. "Everyone, please raise your hands as Yadier did to tell me you can hear me."

Pilar said, "I am..."

Benito said, "Yes, Diego." He sat up to take a close look at Blanca; his eyes were almost swollen shut. Blanca was breathing normally and she was awake. Benito stroked her hair and laid back down next to her.

Without moving, Bernardo said, "Yeah boss, water?"

Diego answered, "Bernardo, all of you, we have a few cans of condensed milk below. Big Bernardo, can you reach it? It will help us all."

He slowly sat up. After a few minutes, he edged to the slot in the deck and reached below. "I got two cans," he said. Then he laid back down on the deck.

"Pilar, Benito," said Diego, "can one of you move this way and steer for a few minutes? I will open the milk and check on Blanca."

BAM! The boat hit bottom and lurched violently to the right. The mast cracked, and the rudder was ripped out of Diego's hands. The crew was tossed to the right, but even without the lifelines they stayed on deck. Everyone sat up.

"The hell?" said Yadier. The rest looked around but it took a moment for them to comprehend what happened.

"We hit a reef," said Diego, "and we are aground. Look in the water. You can see the bottom."

Pilar looked to the west and said, "*Fantastico,* I see land right over there. We are so close."

"Yes, yes, we can swim from here," said Yadier. Although his judgment was clouded, Bernardo and Pilar agreed. Benito was not leaving Blanca.

"I am sorry," said Diego, "but it is much further than it looks, and you are already very weak. You will drown. Please, stay on the boat where you are safe. Another boat will come by and help us."

"We cannot be sure. I say we swim." Yadier was beyond thinking logically.

"No, I beg you. Look, in the distance you can see other boats." Diego's voice was frantic. "This broken chug is our island. Stay with her. Stay with her for an hour. Then you can do what you want."

The wristwatch Diego offered for timing crew shifts had stopped long ago, but he found another timer. "The GPS has a clock, you see? Just one hour." Diego was buying time, hoping for a rescue, a miracle.

Yadier said, "One hour, then we swim to America." Bernardo, Yadier, and Pilar laid back down.

As the hour counted down and the sun got higher in the sky, no other boats came near.

CHAPTER TWENTY-EIGHT

"What's that on your starboard bow, a marker?" asked Jackson.

"I'm not sure," replied Art. "See what the chart says."

Jackson zoomed the GPS image by touching the screen, then he looked at the paper chart. "There is no marker there, but we need to be careful; that is a very shallow spot called Cannon Patch."

As they approached, they could tell it was a wrecked boat of some kind. "Oh my god, there are people aboard. Do you see the guy waving?" asked Jackson.

"Yeah, I am going to approach slowly and watch for debris. Man, we are in skinny water." Art pushed the small lever on the throttle to raise the outdrive. The motor made a familiar, metallic buzzing sound as the engine tilted forward and the propeller was raised to just beneath the water's surface. As if they were towing a washing machine, turbulent water splashed above the boat's elevated propeller. Art looked back to confirm that the cooling water intake ports were still under water. They were, and a pee-stream of cooling water continued flowing out of the engine block. Using the throttle, he maintained a safe distance of ten yards from the wrecked boat. Art knew he could not anchor on the protected coral reef.

Jackson could see four men and one woman. All but the first man were on their knees or sitting. It was clear to him this was a refugee boat most likely from Cuba or perhaps Haiti. From college, Jackson was pretty familiar with German, but his Spanish was just enough to order a *chimichanga*. He shouted in English to the crew of the wrecked boat. "Hello! Can we help you?" he asked.

The man who waved to them spoke. His weary face, his crooked posture and his tattered, soiled white shirt spoke of an arduous journey. "I am Diego. We are six people. We are sick and we need food and water."

"Stand by," Jackson shouted. He turned to Art and asked about supplies on the boat.

"I have four bottles of water and four granola bars in the boat bag. I will get closer so you can toss them across. Tell them."

This drill was similar to the dead-in-the-water boat assists they performed often on San Francisco Bay: Help the others, but don't damage your own boat or fall into the water. Otherwise, you will have <u>bigger</u> problems to solve.

Jackson told Diego, "We will come closer to you. I will toss water bottles and snack bars to you." Diego translated for the others. They nodded their understanding. Art pulled aside the wreck. Jackson pitched over the supplies, then Art pulled his boat away. The crew shared the supplies. Like the others, Blanca was revived somewhat by the food and water.

Art said, "We gotta call this in to the Coasties. We can't do any more to help them."

Just then Diego asked, "Can you take us aboard your boat, please?"

They didn't need to discuss it; Art and Jackson knew they should not. It was far better for the Coast Guard to handle the situation, plus Art's boat didn't have the space. Jackson said, "We are going to radio for help to get you care and medical attention." Diego didn't respond; he knew his rescuers were calling the Coast Guard. He translated for the others. They were too worn out to object.

Art estimated that the nearest Coast Guard station was about twenty-five miles down the Keys at Snake Creek in Islamorada. He checked his cell phone: zero bars. He grabbed the VHF radio. It was already on emergency channel sixteen, so he pressed the talk button and said, "Coast Guard Station Islamorada, Coast Guard Station Islamorada, this is power vessel *Jenny Girl* on channel one-six, over."

Art got a reply. "Vessel *Jenny Girl*, this is Coast Guard Station Islamorada, go ahead, over." Art and Jackson were pleased that the handheld radio transmitted so far.

"Station, *Jenny Girl*. We have encountered a grounded sailing vessel with six persons on board on the ocean side of Key Largo. There are injuries, over."

"*Jenny Girl*, station: please state your position, over."

"Station, this is *Jenny Girl*, our position is Cannon Patch, latitude twenty-five degrees, zero six, point two minutes north; eighty degrees, twenty point six minutes west, over."

"Roger, *Jenny Girl*. We will dispatch a Dolphin medevac helicopter as well as a surface vessel. We request that you remain on scene. When our aircraft arrives, switch to channel twenty-one alpha, so you can coordinate the rescue with the helicopter crew, over."

"Station, wilco, over."

"This is Coast Guard Station Islamorada, out."

Art switched his radio to channel 21A, and Jackson communicated the news to Diego. "Well, they're on their way," said Art. But the Coast Guard weren't the only ones coming.

CHAPTER TWENTY-NINE

As a standard practice, Lenny kept his marine radio aboard *Tinkerbell* tuned to channel sixteen. Lenny and Ed listened to the call from *Jenny Girl*, and Ed recognized the voice. Ed also heard their location. Ed zoomed in on the GPS screen and quickly found Cannon Patch. He marked it as a waypoint in the device. He pushed the GO TO feature and was shown the bearing and distance from their current location.

Ed said, "Look, they're only about ten minutes away. Let's go have a talk with 'em."

"I'll head over there, Ed, but I won't be part of any rough stuff. Do you understand?" Lenny had seen Ed go nuclear before, and he was tired of it.

"Sure, Lenny. I just wanna tell him off a bit, sorta have the last word. Then that's the end of it." Lenny changed course and pushed the throttle forward.

***

"May I come aboard your boat?" Diego asked Jackson. "I have something important to tell you."

Art looked at Jackson and shook his head. "I'm sorry, Diego. We will wait for help from the Coast Guard," said Jackson.

"But I have information critical to the national security of the United States," Diego said.

"Why didn't you simply take this information to our embassy in Havana or just fly out of Cuba like many tourists are doing now?"

"The Cuban government knows I have this information and they are after me. I have been hiding in the countryside for a long time waiting to sneak out of Cuba."

Jackson pressed Diego. "How can we be sure you won't try to hijack our boat?"

"You see me. I am tired and can barely stand. I will take off my clothes to show you I have no weapons," Diego said. "Please, while we wait, let me show you something. It is very important for your country."

Jackson turned to Art and said, "Let's hear him out. He can't overpower us."

"I don't like it, but okay. I will motor over there to pick him up, then we'll stand off in case the others try to storm our boat." Jackson made a thumbs-up gesture to Diego.

"Diego, we are coming to get you," said Jackson. "I will help you step aboard." Jackson hung fenders on the starboard side of the boat, and Art nestled her up against the wooden wreck. Diego clutched Jackson's extended arm and he stepped aboard *Jenny Girl*. Although Diego smelled like a dumpster, the men shook hands.

As Art drove a short distance from the chug, he looked over his shoulder and asked, "So what's this all about?"

Diego gathered himself and explained his unique access to Cuban generals and their plans to acquire Sarin gas. "How do we know this is true?" asked Jackson.

Diego pulled a computer thumb drive from his pocket. He said, "This little memory chip was the most important thing from that wrecked boat, including me. It holds hundreds of documents gathered by me and my medical colleagues who also had high-level access. This information will prove what I just told you. This must get to your Senate's Committee on Foreign Relations. <u>Right now</u> they are considering easing sanctions on Cuba. That would be a terrible, dangerous mistake."

"So," said Art, "why don't you just give it to me, and I will contact my Senator and she will get it to the right people?"

Diego said, "Sir, I not only brought you documents, I am an eyewitness to these discussions about Sarin. I risked my life to carry this personally, and I would like your Senate committee to hear from me directly. So, please…"

The discussion was interrupted by another boat, a Mako, pulling up. It's prop was also high in the water to accommodate the minimum depth. Art and Jackson immediately recognized Ed; he was riding at the back of the boat. The driver was Ed's slender friend from the argument at Mrs. Mac's earlier in the week.

John Gordon

CHAPTER THIRTY

"Well look here, Lenny," said Ed. "We got us a couple Californicators and their Cuban *amigos*. What's all this, a raft-up party? Who's the vagrant on your boat? He's one of the Cubans, right?" said Ed.

"I told you to stay away from me dipshit," said Art. "Get lost before I climb on that boat and put my boot up your ass."

Ed reached into his sea bag and pulled out a pistol. "You were sure tough when there were three of you on me. Now it's two on two plus my friend Mr. Glock."

Tinkerbell remained in gear; Lenny stayed at the helm. From there he said, "Ed, stop. This is bullshit."

Art said, "Put the gun away, Ed. Nobody else is armed, so you don't need the hardware. If you want a rebate on your $300 tire payment, I can do that here and now."

"I'll take the money but first, no goddam Cubans. Chico here's gotta get back on the chug." Ed was adamant.

Jackson stepped forward and in front of Diego. He said, "We're just giving him some water. We'll put him back on the chug when the Coast Guard arrives."

"I said he gets on the chug, now!"

"But Ed…"

BLAM! Ed shot Yadier in the calf. "Now, do you see I'm serious? I say he gets on the chug, <u>now</u>." Benito and the others on the chug moved to care for Yadier. The terror of the shooting was another challenge piled atop their exhaustion and hunger. Pilar and Blanca cried, and Bernardo shouted insults at Ed. Fortunately, Yadier was only grazed.

Once more, Jackson tried reasoning. Ed lifted the gun and pointed it toward Jackson. Jackson spun to pull Diego down, but a second shot caught Jackson in the side. He and Diego flopped to the deck. Jackson was on top of Diego, and he was bleeding badly. Art rushed to check on Jackson. Diego was already attending to him.

"Diego said, "Continue to hold this towel over the wound firmly while I try to clean my filthy hands in the saltwater."

Lenny had seen enough. Without warning, he pushed hard on *Tinkerbell's* throttle. The boat leapt forward, launching Ed head-first over the transom and onto the boat's raised, spinning propeller. Everyone aboard the migrant boat gasped as a pool of blood formed around Ed's body. He was face-up and conscious in the water, but the tissue around his left shoulder had been shredded. He was moaning from the pain.

Lenny had pulled his boat away from the scene while Art and Diego were busy treating Jackson's wound. Ed was left unattended, and he was struggling to keep his head above the surface. Without a word, Bernardo leapt off the chug into the water. He swam the few yards to Ed and he held Ed's head above water.

Bernardo said, "*Relajarse.*" *Relax.* Then Bernardo reached his left arm around Ed's upper torso and he swam sidestroke back to the chug. Pilar and Benito helped Bernardo get Ed onto the chug's deck where Pilar placed a rolled blanket on his bloody shoulder and added pressure. Although Ed was disoriented from his sudden injury and his struggles in the water, he was aware that he was aboard the chug, being aided by the Cubans. *Blanket, yes. Holy shit. I'm on a pile of piss-smelling scrap lumber with a bunch of Cubans. Shoulder hurts like hell. I'm gonna bleed to death here and the last words I hear are gonna be "Adios amigo." Why're they helpin' me? I coulda sworn I winged one of them. Sun feels good. What's wrong with these people! I shot one, yeah. They're lookin' at me. Yeah, bueno, bueno.*

On Art's boat, Jackson was awake but hurting badly. "Hey Jackie," said Art, "I hear the helo coming in, so just relax. You're gonna be just fine. You'll be surfing clean sheets in fifteen minutes." Jackson looked at Ed and Diego, but he said nothing. He was pale.

With the helicopter nearing, Art pulled his new, red West Marine jacket from the boat bag and said, "Diego, doc, put this on. You're going with him." Diego flashed a confused look. Art just nodded and helped him with the jacket.

Diego took over with Jackson. Art could hear the helo trying to reach him on the radio. Art scurried to the helm and talked with the helicopter crew before they were directly overhead. Art could barely hear them, so he shouted into the radio so they could hear him.

"Yes, this is vessel *Jenny Girl*, we need you more urgently now. We have a person aboard my boat who has been shot and another person on a grounded wooden sailboat whose shoulder has been slashed by a propeller."

"Vessel *Jenny Girl*, Coast Guard 6596, Roger," said the helicopter crewman working communications. "Is the shooter still active?"

Art responded, "The shooter is a white male, disarmed, and no longer a threat. He is the injured man on the sailboat."

"Roger Captain. We will notify the Monroe County Sheriff's Office of the shooting. What are the shooting victim's injuries and condition?"

Art said, "The shooting victim is conscious. We are applying pressure to the wound in his abdomen."

"Roger. How many persons need immediate Medivac?" asked comms.

"Three people will come aboard, the shooting victim and his doctor plus the badly injured shooter."

The comms person said, "*Jenny Girl*, Coast Guard 6596, Station advised there were six persons on board needing assistance."

"Negative. The other people need food and water but I believe they are well enough to wait for your surface vessel," said Art.

"*Jenny Girl*, 6596, Roger. We have multiple vessels in sight. Request you signal from the vessels with the persons being evacuated. The Coast Guard boat will arrive in less than fifteen minutes."

Art waved both arms above his head. He shouted to the chug for someone to also wave to the helicopter pilot. Benito waved. Then Art said, "Roger, the Coast Guard boat arrives in less than fifteen minutes, over."

"*Jenny Girl*, 6596, when we are overhead the light green power vessel, we will lower a rescue swimmer. He will assist you with the rescue basket."

"Roger," said Art. "You will lower a rescue swimmer, then the rescue basket."

Soon, the massive orange helo was overhead; the noise from the engine was deafening. The crew quickly lowered an orange-clad rescue swimmer wearing a white helmet to the boat. He unbuckled the cable and sent it back up. Soon the rescue basket was lowered. The swimmer eased it to the boat's deck. Then Art and the swimmer helped Diego climb into the basket.

The rescue swimmer shouted, "Who is this?"

"He is the doctor. He must go with the shooting victim," yelled Art. He knew that if Diego didn't get on first, the swimmer and the copter might leave with only Jackson and Ed, the injured boaters.

The swimmer paused, then he gave a thumbs-up to a crewman at the door of the helo. The basket went skyward until it reached the doorway. It was pulled inside where Diego climbed out. The basket was lowered again without delay. The swimmer and Art gently placed Jackson in the basket.

Before Jackson was hoisted to the helicopter, Art kneeled very close to him and loudly said, "I'll see you in the hospital. You're a tough guy. You've got this."

After Jackson was aboard the helo, the rescue swimmer pointed and shouted to the chug. "Is that the man with the shoulder injury?" he asked.

Benito didn't fully understand the question, but he pointed to Ed and said "Si, si."

The swimmer dove into the water and glided to the chug. He climbed aboard and checked Ed's injury. *Not good.* He shouted to Ed, "Hello. I am going to help you into a basket, then you will be lifted to that helicopter for evacuation. Got it?" Ed managed a slight nod.

The swimmer waved to the helicopter pilot, then the aircraft moved directly above him. They lowered the basket again. The swimmer and Benito helped Ed into the basket, and it was lifted to the helo. Inside the helicopter, Ed was placed on the deck not far from Jackson. In their traumatized state, neither was aware of the other. Of course, Diego knew about them both.

After Diego and the two injured men were aboard, the helicopter lowered the cable, and the swimmer took the last ride up. Then the helicopter flew forward, gained altitude and headed for south Miami. Finally it was quiet at the scene. While Jackson, Art, and Diego had waited for helicopter rescue, Lenny and his boat had returned. He spoke passable Spanish, so he explained to the remaining huddled and shocked immigrants waiting on the chug that they would soon be safe aboard a Coast Guard boat. Their tense faces and darting eyes revealed their terror.

Lenny felt horrible about injuring his friend, but he had no regrets about the action he took. Still, it was gruesome and painful to see Ed bloodied in the water. He thought about the many times they boated together and how much fun they had. Lenny also thought about Ed's daughter, Tina, and how she would react to her dad's injury and arrest. It was an awful message, but he resolved to call Tina as soon as he got home.

All aboard the three clustered vessels were silent. They heard only the sparkling water of the Florida Straits gently splashing against the boats and the squawking of seagulls circling overhead. After a short while, a Coast Guard patrol boat appeared in the distance.

CHAPTER THIRTY-ONE

"Hey big boy, you want some company in that bed?"

Jackson had been dozing. He slowly directed his eyes to the door and saw his wife. "Are you an angel or are you my beautiful bride?" It was a corny line, but it was the best he could do under the pain meds.

Sharon walked briskly to his bed and kissed him. "You look pretty good for a target," she said. She pursed her lips, then tears ran down her cheeks. Emotions and fatigue had caught up with her. *Darn, I wanted to stay upbeat through all this.*

"Babe, I am fine. Don't let the saline drip and the heart monitor concern you," said Jackson. His voice was groggy. "I can't tell you how happy I am to see you."

Art had been waiting outside Jackson's private room to allow them a little time alone. He entered the room. It was bright due to the sizable window overlooking a vast parking lot. The walls were freshly painted; the speckled tile floor was spotless. There were colorful Florida scenes decorating the walls. Unlike many other hospitals, the furnishings didn't look like Kmart blue-light specials.

"So you like Florida so much you will pull a stunt like this to stay longer? How are you feeling, Jackie?" asked Art.

"Much better now that I have beauty and the beast here in my room. Are you two gonna start singing? Please don't."

Art pulled over a chair for Sharon and he grabbed one for himself. Jackson asked Sharon, "How did you get here so fast. It's Sunday, right?"

Sharon said, "Yes, it's about 4:45 PM on Sunday. As for how I got here, Art called and told me the situation after he got back to his house. I booked a nonstop redeye on American. It was 7:30 AM when I got to Miami. I took an Uber to a hotel near here to get some sleep and let you rest longer. Then Art picked me up, and here we are."

"Wow. I am <u>so</u> glad you are here," said Jackson, "and thank you, Art, for helping Sharon with all this."

Sharon waved her hand and said, "Enough about logistics, give me a medical update. I am so pleased to see you looking so good. I was really worried, even though Art kept saying you'd be fine."

"You probably know I was brought here by a Coast Guard helicopter. This place…"

"Jackson Memorial Hospital," said Art.

"Yes," said Jackson. "How weird is that? Jackson Boyd in Jackson Memorial Hospital? It's like they already dedicated the place to me." Sharon knew it was the meds talking.

Just then a nurse poked in her head and asked, "Mr. Boyd, you need anything? How about you folks?"

"No thanks, Nurse Parker," said Jackson. Then he said to his visitors, "Where was I?"

Sharon said, "You arrived by Coast Guard helicopter."

"Yes, then a flock of triage people asked a lot of questions, and they looked at my wound, and they rolled me over, and they checked my vitals. Then they took me to a room where I was prepped for the ER. Oh wait, they x-rayed me to look at the bullet and the internal damage before surgery. Hey, shouldn't a group called 'triage' be three people?"

"Sure," said Art. "How long was the surgery?"

"I wasn't sure, but they told me an hour. They said sometimes they leave the bullet in, but they took out mine."

A doctor peeked into the room. "I'm sorry to interrupt. I am Dr. Thomas Andrews. I performed the surgery. Okay if I check you, Mr. Boyd?" Jackson nodded.

Dr. Andrews was tall and handsome. He had an easy smile and thinning blond hair that was cut very short. His lab coat was freshly pressed and spotless. Dr. Andrews had the look Central Casting would send if your movie needed a distinguished-looking lawyer, congressman, or doctor.

Dr. Andrews said to the visitors, "You are welcome to stay. I just need to get to his left side." Art and Sharon pulled their chairs back, and the doctor stepped forward. Jackson slowly rolled so the doctor could pull away the dressing and examine the wound. "Looking good," said Dr. Andrews. "What is your pain level, Mr. Boyd?"

"Much better than before," said Jackson. "On a scale of zero to ten, I'd say a three."

"I'm glad to hear that," said Dr. Andrews. He put the bandages back and said, "I'll ask your nurse to replace that dressing in an hour or so."

"Thanks doc," said Jackson.

"One more thing," said the doctor, "on your x-ray I saw something else. It was vague, but I am guessing it's a peptic ulcer. Have you been experiencing any stomach discomfort?"

"Only every day, all day," said Jackson.

"I'm sorry to hear that, but I think we can take care of it," he said. "We'll perform a special test where you swallow some quasi-tasty liquid containing barium while we take x-rays to have a better look. If it _is_ a peptic ulcer, we can use special antibiotics to solve the problem."

"I am so relieved," said Jackson, "I thought I was looking at some slice-and-dice when I got back home. Thank you, doctor." Sharon and Art were relieved as well. They thanked the doctor.

Sharon said, "Dr. Andrews, I am Jackson's wife, Sharon. Thank you for the fine care he is receiving. Would you tell me about his internal injuries from the bullet?" Despite everyone's attempts at keeping the mood light, Sharon was very worried.

"Yes, certainly," said the doctor. "From what he told the folks in receiving, he twisted his upper torso just before he was shot. By doing so, he narrowed his silhouette, so the bullet only caught flesh. No vital organs were involved, thankfully. I removed the bullet without much difficulty."

Art exhaled loudly, and Sharon said, "Oh my God, doctor. I can't thank you enough." She wanted to hug him.

Art asked, "So how long will he be here?"

"Most likely a week. We want to closely monitor the healing process and watch for infection. I think we cleaned the wound very well, but sometimes small particles and debris from clothing or the environment get introduced into the body in a situation like this." He paused for other questions, then he said, "Let the staff know if you desire more information. They can always reach me, and I will phone you back as soon as I can." He smiled and left the room. Jackson, Sharon and Art thanked him again as he walked away.

Jackson said, "Oh, Sharon, my favorite yellow boating shirt was sorta stained, plus it was cut off me. I'm afraid it's gone forever."

"Sweetie, I know you liked that shirt, and you know I <u>hated</u> that shirt. So, let's just call it even, okay? When you are back home, we will get you another 'favorite shirt'," she said.

Jackson smiled, then he addressed Art. "What happened on the boat after I boarded the flying orange bus?"

"The Coastie patrol boat arrived fifteen minutes after the helo left, maybe less. They put the immigrants aboard their boat to get them out of the sun. They gave them food and Gatorade, and they performed first aid on those who needed it. One woman was unconscious but apparently her vitals were stable. They patched up the guy who was grazed by Ed's first shot. That's what they told me anyway."

Art continued, "All the immigrants were to be taken for medical treatment, mostly for exposure and dehydration. The Coasties said that after medical care and being interviewed about the shootings, they would be cared for by Migration and Refugee Services in Miami while their cases were being heard. That is run, they said, by the U.S. Conference of Catholic Bishops."

Jackson interrupted. "That reminds me, on the helicopter, I vaguely remember Diego asking if I could find one of the immigrants named Bernardo and give him $100. I guess Diego had to bribe him to do something important. Diego said if Bernardo hadn't done it they would have died. Now I know where to find Bernardo once I get outta here."

"Just after the Coasties got there, a Monroe County Sheriff's boat arrived," said Art. "One of the crew members said that the Coast Guard helicopter crew contacted them after I reported a shooting on the water. They said, 'the Coast Guard performs rescues; we perform the investigations.' Crew members aboard the Sheriff's boat took photos at the scene and asked Lenny and me a few basic questions. Then we followed them in our boats to a dock near the Sheriff's substation in Tavernier—that's between Key Largo and Islamorada. We went inside for lengthy interviews and formal statements. The authorities asked us to stay in the area for ten days. They said they might question witnesses further after they have a chance to process evidence."

Art turned toward Sharon and said. "I called you after all that. Until we were done, they preferred we didn't make phone calls, plus I wouldn't have had the time to give you details."

"I understand, Art," she said, "you have been pretty busy over the past twenty-four hours. You probably got less sleep than me."

"It's all good, I'll rest tonight," Art replied. "I'm glad you made it here, and I am relieved that Superman here will recover fully." Then Art asked Jackson, "Do you know what the Coasties did with Diego?"

"I remained conscious during the entire flight here, though things are sometimes a bit hazy," said Jackson. "The helo crew members suspected Diego was an immigrant, so they started asking questions. He told them the truth and shared with them what he told us: the Cuban Sarin threat and the documents he had on a thumb drive to prove it. I lied and said I had verified his story—thank goodness they didn't ask how—and that he needed special consideration for our national defense. I said he was so important, I protected him from Ed, the shooter. Again I lied. I tried to get the hell out of the way, and I instinctively pulled Diego down with me. It's not like I threw myself on a live grenade."

Art said, "You did plenty, my friend. So where is Diego now?"

"I can't be sure, but the helicopter pilot said something like he knew personally a member of the Florida House of Representatives; she lives in Key Largo and he would contact her and hand Diego over to her if she was willing to get involved. She could work with her contacts and get him in front of the right people in D.C., something like that."

"That's incredible," said Art. "That pilot took a big risk just bringing Diego onboard the helo. He is also violating federal policy by handing an immigrant over to a private citizen, even though she is an elected state representative. I wonder how that will work out."

Jackson said, "None of us can predict that, but I do know that Diego was still on the helicopter when it lifted off the helipad here. The Coasties hadn't brought ICE here anyway. Someone <u>had</u> contacted the Miami Police Department, however. There were three husky uniformed officers on the helipad when I was taken off first. They verified who I was, then they waited 'to see Mr. Melnik'."

Art asked Jackson, "Were you aware that Ed was on the helicopter with you?"

"Sort of," said Jackson. "I should say I was aware of another injured person. I didn't know who it was. I didn't look at him. During the flight, he cried and mumbled to Diego over and over that he was sorry. That was Ed?"

"Yeah, that was Ed. After the bastard shot you, he took a header onto the other boat's prop, compliments of his friend, Lenny. A big guy from the chug pulled him out of the water. I'm sure Ed is here somewhere getting his shoulder rebuilt before going to jail. It's pretty freaking ironic that a Cuban refugee saved his sorry ass."

Sharon was tired and somewhat shaken by the new details. She said to Art, "We should go, let Jackson get some rest. For all he's been through, he looks good, but tired."

"Yes, I'm very tired," said Jackson, "but promise me you'll come back tomorrow morning."

"Done," said Art, "we'll be here." They both stood. Sharon said her goodbye, kissed Jackson and headed for the door. Art stayed behind.

When Sharon stepped into the hallway, she saw a fortyish-looking woman with short brown hair and a Florida tan approaching quickly. The woman seemed frightened, in a hurry. She slowed as she passed Sharon and she asked, "Do you know where room 5190 is? I've gotta find my dad."

Sharon was moved, probably due to exhaustion and her own sadness at seeing Jackson injured. She said, "No, I'm sorry, but good luck. Hope he's okay."

The woman continued walking, and over her shoulder she said, "Thank you. I'm afraid we're gonna be here a while. Maybe I'll see you again. My name is Tina." She turned a corner and disappeared. Sharon waited outside Jackson's room for Art.

Art stepped closer and handed Jackson a package the size of a square coaster and an inch thick. He said, "This is your medal. Every hero deserves a medal."

Jackson was surprised and curious. He opened the box and the wrapping inside. The gift was contained in a plastic sleeve. Jackson tipped the sleeve and an irregularly shaped silver coin the size of a half-dollar slid into his hand. Its markings were nearly worn away, but Jackson could make out a cross, a scalloped border and some smaller images.

"This is cool. Exactly what is it?" asked Jackson.

"Remember we talked about Mel Fisher finding the Spanish galleon *Atocha*?" Jackson nodded. "That is an eight-Reales coin from that ship. I got it for you today from a reputable jewelry store in Key Largo."

As tired and medicated as he was, Jackson was flabbergasted. "Art, thank you so much. What an extraordinary piece of history; I am thrilled. Oh my. Thank you again, but I hope you got a good deal on it."

Art leaned close to Jackson. His face was serious. He said, "You deserve that and more. I am honored to be your friend. What you did yesterday was the bravest thing I have ever seen. Now get some rest."

Art turned and left the room. Jackson closed his eyes, smiled and fell asleep.

***

ACKNOWLEDGMENTS

The author would like to thank the following people for their
contributions to this book:

Editor and Story Consultant
Gloria Collins

Technical Expertise
Joseph Kirby
Paul Verveniotis

Inspiration
Don Jackson

ABOUT THE AUTHOR

John Gordon is a retired businessman and avid boater. He is a veteran and he served fourteen years as a volunteer U.S. Coast Guard search and rescue boat skipper. John and his wife, Julie, have five children and two grandchildren. They split their time between the San Francisco Bay Area and Key Largo, Florida. This is John's eighth book. Visit johngordon.org for more about John and his projects.

BOOKS BY JOHN GORDON

Jackson Boyd Series
Crash Course
Bloody Waters
Drug Island

Bite-Sized Reads
Bad Altitude
Miss Fit
Manure
Awestruck

Out of Print
Memorable Scenes from an Ordinary Life
Over Seas

www.ingramcontent.com/pod-product-compliance
Lightning Source LLC
Chambersburg PA
CBHW061440150726
47987CB00001B/280